CW00747729

Acknowledgements

I would like to say a massive thank you to everyone who listened, helped and supported while I wrote this book. Especially to Alicia Brunskill for your patient proof reading and editing and Bob Woodcock for your help with the cover. And of course Dan who suffered my ramblings while I banged on about this to him, whether he was really listening or not. There's no way this would be half as good without you guys.

Dedication

This book is for all the people with disabilities out there who try so hard and have so much to offer but aren't understood or given a chance to shine. My hope is that all your skills and qualities will be recognized and that we can push understanding and acceptance forward.

Moving forward

Childhood

I

Jimmy sat at his desk in the busy, noisy, year nine classroom. His pen hovered over the last sentence within the thought cloud printed on the page.

Want to work in films.

He had written. His teacher had told him to write three things in the bubble but racking his brain he couldn't think of what else to add. He underlined the sentence for the third time, put his head on his hand and stared down at page forty of his person centred planning booklet, willing words to come.

Just then, someone knocked at the door.

"Come in!" Mrs Samson, the senior teaching assistant in charge for the hour called over the noise. The door opened and Jimmy looked up to see Miss Fields, a twenty three year old teaching assistant from New Zealand, poke her head round the door. She smiled at Mrs Samson then quickly scanned her eyes over the eleven students and seven other teaching assistants.

"Jimmy Tiffin? Time for your transition review honey," she called to the class.

"Okay," Jimmy said, averting his eyes from Miss Fields and looking back at the page, his pen hovering above the vast amounts of empty space for a few seconds before he had a brainwave and wrote:

Have big house with my wife.

He underlined this sentence three times like the last one, using quick definite strokes of his pen that he couldn't quite keep straight, almost ending up effectively crossing out the words he'd written.

"Jimmy? You ready?" Miss Fields asked, now focused on him. She tilted her head to one side so her thick, curly hair reached her shoulder.

"Ready for what?" Jimmy asked, looking back up.

"To come to your review, honey."

"What's a review honey?"

"It's where they…you talk about how you're doing in school."

"Okay. And why is there honey?"

"There isn't honey. That's sometimes what I call people."

"Okay. Can you call me Jimmy?"

"Yes. Sorry Jimmy. Come on bud, I'm supposed to take you on down there now."

"Okay. Why are you now saying I'm a part of a flower?"

"It's short for buddy," Miss Fields said, her fingers starting to tap impatiently on the door frame. "Come on, let's get going."

"But it's art time next."

"Not today it's not. Today it's review time."

Jimmy looked to Mrs Samson, who nodded at him, so reluctantly he started to pack away his things into his rucksack.

When he was ready, they said goodbye to Mrs Samson and the rest of the class, then Miss Fields took his hand and they started walking together down the bright corridors. She set a quick, uncomfortable pace.

"Why are you holding my hand?" Jimmy asked, a question that he often found himself asking.

"Because…because it's safer."

"But we are in school. We are safe. There are no cars," Jimmy said, looking ahead at the silver rimmed clock and the time that made him slightly uncomfortable. Three minutes past two. It was supposed to be art time, not review time.

"Because…because I'm supposed to."

"But teachers of my brother who is one year and seven months and two days younger than me do not hold his hand. He said so. He said it is because I run away."

"Well there you go then."

"But why might I run away? I have autism; does that mean I run away?"

"Some people do, yes."

"But I do not do running away. Where would I go?"

"I don't know Jimmy. I don't know. But I'm holding your hand and that's that," Miss Fields said with a quiet sigh.

"But why do you do it if you do not know why you do it?"

"Leave it Jimmy," she sighed, exasperatedly.

"Oh. Okay," said Jimmy, resigned. "Sorry Miss Fields.

"That's okay mate," she said softly, "but you do ask a lot of questions."

They reached the entrance to the teacher's offices a few moments later and Miss Fields had to let go of his hand to punch in the four digit code to the staff rooms. Jimmy felt his heart quicken a bit as she did, those were rooms he went through so seldom and never un-escorted.

On the other side of the door Miss Fields took his hand up again and they walked down the corridor to the head teacher's office, where she knocked upon the door.

"Yes?" called Mrs Dorite from inside her room; using a sweeter more sing song tone then Jimmy remembered her having.

"It's us," Miss Fields called back.

"One minute please," came the reply.

"Okay," Miss Fields called, then leaned her shoulder against the wall and glanced down at her watch.

A minute went by. Then another thirty seconds. Another minute and seven seconds passed. Jimmy was getting really nervous.

"Have you seen Elf?" He asked. "It was on TV."

"No I haven't, is it good?"

"It is about an Elf who goes into a Coffee shop and says well done because they have a sign that says world's best cup of coffee in the window and so he says well done."

"Oh. Okay. Does it have a good ending?"

"The end is about when some people sing Santa Claus is coming to town."

"Okay... and why do they sing that?"

"Because they do."

"Right."

"It is a good film."

"Good," Miss Fields said, trying to disguise a yawn.

Another minute went by and Jimmy could feel himself trembling. He didn't know what was going on behind the closed door, but whatever it was he wished he could just go in, get it out of the way and go back to class. Until, yet another minute later, when Mrs Dorite's voice came loudly from inside:

"We're ready for you now!"

Miss Fields could finally let them in.

Inside were many wooden tables pushed together to make one long one which was surrounded by a lot of people; most of whom he didn't recognize, all of whom were looking up at him and smiling. Jimmy felt himself tense up, almost reaching for Miss Fields hand, before remembering his age and why he had such a problem with that in the first place.

"Hi Jimmy," the assembled group chorused.

Jimmy didn't answer. He just stood in the doorway, looking down at the table littered with paper headed with his name, and mugs of half-drunk coffee and tea.

"Jimmy, would you like to take a seat by your mum?" Mrs Dorite asked. Jimmy didn't move until a moment later when he realised that Miss Fields had slipped back out the door, leaving him on his own.

"Jimmy, come sit down," his mum called to him, patting the empty chair next to her.

He moved slowly over to the chair, drew it about a foot back from the table and sat down.

"Right then Jimmy, this is your transition review!" Mrs Dorite said from her place at the head of the table. "It is a review to look at your future, *'cos you won't be here with us forever!*" She told him, laughing at this for reasons Jimmy didn't understand. "I'll be chairing the meeting and these people around the table," she waved her hand in a circle, "are people who are here to help and support you as you become an adult. As you know, I'm Mrs Dorite, head teacher here at Hollygroves School."

She then motioned to her left at a thirty something man wearing smart jeans and a plain, red t-shirt.

"Jimmy, I'm Dave Heddon from the local authority. It's my job to help young people like you move into adulthood. I'll be helping you to gain independence and develop your social skills."

"I'm Gene Trod from Connexions," the lady to his left said. Jimmy recognized the accent as Welsh, like his neighbors.

"You know me!" said Mrs Gregory, Jimmy's class teacher.

"And me!" Jimmy's Mum said out of turn.

"And I'm Daniel Graves," said the man to Mrs Gregory's left, "I'm a trainee social worker and will be taking over from Shamsun as your family's allocated case worker."

"And I'm Shamsun," the lady to his left said, "we've met a couple of times before haven't we Jimmy?"

Jimmy had thought he had seen her face before, but hadn't been able to place it at first. She had come round a few times to help them 'adapt' the house for him. Putting schedules up on walls or using software on the computers to write so that pictures appeared above the words to make things easier for Jimmy to understand. His family had always taken her advice to heart, with the best intentions, but as soon as they'd forgotten once or twice to update the schedule or the picture symbols Jimmy became uncomfortable. He didn't like seeing a wrong schedule on the wall or the wrong picture above a word. Eventually the practice would start to fall apart until they just gave up.

"Now Jimmy, we've just been talking about you and how well you're doing at school," Mrs Dorite said to him. "Do you enjoy school Jimmy?"

Jimmy wasn't sure what to say to this. He did a lot at school, some things he liked, some things he didn't. But everyone was looking at him so he took a gamble and nodded.

"Excellent!" Mrs Dorite said, clasping her hands together. "What's your favorite thing about school?"

"I like art," he said, surprised and confused at the sound of his own voice coming out croaky, "and project. I like project because I got to do work with film."

"Yes, the films," Mrs Dorite said tittering with a knowing look on her face.

"Now Jimmy, what do you think you'd like to do after school?" The man who'd introduced himself as Dave asked him.

"I'd like to go home and watch a film and have a snack," Jimmy said.

"No, I mean when School's finished."

"Yes. I'd like to watch a film at home," Jimmy said, looking up at the man, wondering why he didn't get it.

"No, I mean when you stop going to school altogether. When you're nineteen and an adult? Would you, for instance, like to go to a post nineteen special needs College? One you'd sleep at, like if you went to a university. Or maybe you'd like to work?" Dave said, smiling at him.

"I'd like to work with films."

"You'd like to be an actor?"

"No. I'd like to be a director or a camera man or a producer," Jimmy answered, happy now to be able to talk about something he loved to talk about.

"Well now," Mrs Dorite said to him, "that'd be great, in a perfect world. But we've just been talking about how well you were doing in cookery and in Café."

"He makes great cups of tea and sandwiches at home," Jimmy's Mum chimed in.

"Well now, did you here that?" Mrs Dorite exclaimed. "Gene, are there many post nineteen colleges that provide catering courses?"

"Oh, loads!" Gene said beaming. "There's a residential provision called Hayden that has a great catering course, one of the best."

"Oh wow, that sounds perfect, eh Jimmy?" Mrs Dorite said.

"I want to work in films," Jimmy answered.

"Well, maybe that would be something you could do on the side, like a club," Mrs Dorite said whilst making notes on a piece of paper before her. Jimmy looked up to watch her writing. Just under 'To stay in our post sixteen sixth form' she had written, 'skills for life/ catering course' and circled it three times.

"Well the next step then Mrs Tiffin is to start looking at prospectuses for colleges and maybe make a visit or two. These residential places are popular and the funding process takes a while to get through, although generally coming from Hollygroves, the funding council understand that students probably do need the extra support of a specialized provision."

"That's good," Jimmy's mum said nodding.

"So you want to have your name on waiting lists in the next couple of years," Gene continued.

"Well, that sounds doable, eh Jim?" His mum said, giving him a playful nudge.

"Right, so that's on track," Mrs Dorite said to the table. "But Jimmy, we've also been talking about social opportunities for you, to build up social skills and independence skills. Now the summer holidays aren't too far away and Dave had a very interesting idea for you."

"That's right Jimmy. What do you like doing in the summer holidays?" Dave asked.

Jimmy didn't answer; again he didn't fully understand the question. He knew that it was one of those questions where you were supposed to pick out the key points to tell people. But what were the key points? Sometimes they went on holiday, they visited Grandma. He watched films and read books and went on the internet. During his last summer holiday Dad and him had had a project in which they painted the garage and the bathroom.

But it didn't matter because before he could start thinking about key points Dave interrupted the process.

"Well, we run holiday groups where people, like yourself, go out and about in the community with lots of lovely support staff. They go swimming, bowling and on trains to the sea side. Would you like to do that?"

"That sounds great!" Jimmy's mum said. "There you go Jimmy; that will fill up your time, save you from watching those films over and over!"

"Right, sounds good. So you'll send the family the paperwork Dave?" Mrs Dorite said.

"Yep, no problem."

"Excellent!" She exclaimed. "Well, that all seems sorted. Would you like to go back to class Jimmy?"

Jimmy, who had been trying to listen to what they were saying, but who was so confused by the amount of information, just nodded.

"Right. Miss Fields?" She called loudly.
The door opened again and in she came.

"Can you take Jimmy back to class now?"

"Course," Miss Fields said nodding and holding out her hand for Jimmy.

"Do I have to do holding your hand?" He asked.

"Yes bud," Miss Fields told him.

"But I won't run away."

"Come on Jimmy, you know you have to hold her hand," His mum said.

"Okay," said Jimmy, "but I don't know why I need to." Jimmy stood up.

"Bye Jimmy!" The table chorused.

"See you in the summer!" Dave called as Jimmy took the hovering hand and let Miss Fields lead him out the room and into the corridor.

Back in his classroom, the art lesson was winding down and everyone had begun packing away their things ready for Project.

"Where were you?" Robert asked as Jimmy went and sat in-between his friends.

"At a transition annual review," Jimmy replied.

"What is that?" Robert asked.

"It was a review to talk about my future."

"Yeah! That's great dude!" Robert exclaimed.

"Yes."

"Dude! And are you going to do working in films dude?" Aalap asked from Jimmy's other side.

"Yes. But I don't know when. They did not help me know that. I think I am going to do college," Jimmy told him.

"Okay dude," Aalap said.

"And I am going swimming in the summer with Dave. Are you going swimming in the summer as well?"

"I don't know dude," Aalap said, "I think so dude. Maybe dude."

"Oh. That's good," Jimmy said, getting his things out from his bag for project, "that is good."

2

Sally got home from school at around four, opened up the door with her key and headed on inside. She put her bag down and fed her cat, Sammy, then went through and sat on the fading, grey sofa and switched on the TV. She resisted the urge to watch cartoons and turned instead to a soap opera she didn't fully understand. Her Mum wasn't in, which meant she was round a friend's or in the pub already.

At five Sally picked Sammy up from her lap and put him on the sofa. Then she went into the small kitchen and moved one of the hard, wooden chairs underneath the shelves that her dad had put up when he was still around; that was over nine years ago. Scraping it along the dusty floor she noticed a layer of crumbs. She'd sweep them up later. Her mum knew she would, that's why she left them.

Once she'd moved the chair she stood on it so that she could reach her hand onto the top shelf. The only shelf where she could put things without them becoming instantly buried under a cascade of bills, pizza menus and taxi cards. This is where she kept the recipes that she cut or tore out of her mum's magazines.

She pulled down the thirty six pages then stepped gingerly off the chair back onto the dirty floor. She took the recipes into the lounge, cleared a large space on the wooden table and put them down carefully. She started working her way through them, separating the ones she had looked at into a new pile, keeping in mind what she could make with the food at her disposal. She knew there were eggs in the fridge, her mum couldn't have used twelve in two days. There was always pasta and bacon and she had cream and onions in her special hiding spot, within the vegetable tray at the bottom of the fridge. After running the ingredients through her mind she decided on Spaghetti Carbonara. Sally stood up stiffly, feeling the cold. She decided to switch the heating on to try and warm the house. Then, smiling, she started setting up in the kitchen. This was her favorite part of the day.

First she took down a large mixing bowl from one of the shelves then scrubbed at the dried on foods that had set around the rim. Once clean, she placed the bowl on the kitchen work surface in a space she had just cleared next to the recipe that, like the others she chose, had step by step pictures as well as words.

This done she took out all the ingredients she needed and lined them up on the side. She measured each ingredient for the sauce to the ml or gram and put them into bowls. Next she chopped the bacon and onion taking great care to avoid cutting herself, which she used to do by accident when she was younger and attempting this sort of thing. With a pencil she ticked off each ingredient once prepared, she would erase the tiny marks later.

Sally checked the recipe then selected the ingredients for the sauce and mixed them clockwise in the bowl, just like the picture suggested. Once blended, she put the mixture to one side. She consulted the recipe again then put the spaghetti sticks into a large pan on the hob. Next she put the plastic kettle on to boil, stepping back a pace so she could watch it bubble through the thin Perspex strip. Taking the recipe and her pencil again she ticked off the instructions like she had the ingredients. When the water had boiled she slowly poured it on the pasta and turned on the hob.

She then poured a tablespoon of oil into a frying pan and put it next to the boiling spaghetti. Exactly ten minutes later she turned on the heat. As soon as the oil bubbled she added the onion and bacon. She stepped back to read the recipe and tick off more instructions then waited. She checked her digital watch continuously until, finally, four minutes was up.

The pasta cooked, she drained it and added it to the frying pan; just avoiding scalding herself as she did. Then she added the sauce, stirring constantly so that it all cooked thoroughly and waited the five minutes written in the instructions before she turned off the heat and fetched herself a plate.

She half poured, half spooned the mixture onto it and took a step back to admire her creation. The food looked good. Sally loved to see the way the individual components could be turned into something else by following a simple, step by step routine. She frowned; something was wrong. It took her a minute to realize what it was: the pan was still three quarters full of food, she had made far too much! If her mum saw the extra food it would mean a lecture about wasting things and how they weren't 'made of money.' Sally knew that people weren't made of money so she never understood why her mum said this. Sally's mum didn't understand that although she could follow recipes happily she had to follow them exactly, often making meals for four or even six. With her heart pounding she held the heavy pan over the bin and poured away about half of what was left then hid it under a cascade of kitchen towels; just in case her mum glanced in. Now she could relax. She put the pan back on the stove with a lid on, like she'd been shown, so it would keep for when her mum returned.

She ate in front of the television with a cushion on her lap and her plate on top of that, watching a teen drama she enjoyed. The episode that evening was about a party the main teenaged characters held and the day afterwards when they found most of the house had been wrecked. She liked watching all the teens in their groups and their cliques, getting into trouble with teachers and parents (like she did) and partying (like she wished she did) all of them doing it together. Friends spending time with friends. Just like she wished she could.

The closest she had felt to having a true friend was Mel. Mel and her used to go out every week on Thursdays. They'd go bowling, ride buses, go shopping for clothes and jewelry that Sally would wear with pride, having this beautiful, fashionable brunette picking it out for her. Mel would stand up for her when people talked down to her, when she was having trouble paying for things, working out change or bus numbers.

She knew how to keep Sally's occasionally quick temper cooled with her stories or getting her cups of tea when the bowling lanes broke and Sally was half way through her go.

But Mel had only lasted three months with her before she got a full time job and couldn't do her part time one anymore. Sally still saw her occasionally at the disabled team's functions, but it wasn't like it used to be. She hadn't left numbers or even accepted Sally on facebook, though Sally kept asking. But that was what friends did, wasn't it? The whole thing had confounded her so much that she could never really settle with the next succession of appointed 'friends' until they said they couldn't match her with anyone anymore. She'd been in trouble for wandering off from some or arguing with others, but when she'd run away from the last one it had been the final straw.

It wasn't her fault. Or she was sure it wasn't, she never meant to run away, it just sort of happened. It was with Amy, while they were on their way to the cinema. Amy was the new girl, sixteen years old to Sally's thirteen, very well spoken and neatly dressed with a pointy little nose and a black bob of hair. Sally never warmed to her.

It had started as they were getting on the 721 bus into town and Sally realized she'd left her 'freedom pass' back at the house.

"Do you want us to go back and get the pass?" Amy had asked, pronouncing every syllable of each word.

"No. I will do paying two pounds," said Sally, taking her little pink purse out of her jeans and opening up the change compartment.

She started rooting around, trying to find the money but she couldn't find what she was looking for.

"Any time today," the driver said impatiently as he closed the doors to the bus.

She stared into her purse. She knew she had two pounds in there, but she couldn't find the coins that she recognized; the ones she'd learnt about in school. Her purse was full of silver, but no gold and no fifty pence pieces. She took out a few of the coins, daring to hope and put them in the driver's outstretched hand.

"This is forty five pence," he said, looking at Amy, "you're short."

"I've got it," Amy said quickly and handed him over a two pound coin. "Your mum can pay me back later. Come on, let's sit down."

"I…I c…c…could ha…have…paid," Sally said, each stuttered word frustrating her further.

"Okay Sally. Next time remember your freedom pass please," Amy said in a whiney tone that sounded like Sally's least favourite teacher.

They took the first seats they saw, Sally by the wheelchair space and Amy just behind her.

Sally was fuming already, trying to calm herself by staring out the window and noticing familiar road signs, when an old man with a stick, who'd got on at the last stop, came and stood next to her. She glanced at him quickly then turned her attention back to the roads.

"You going to just sit there?" The man asked a minute later.

Sally turned to him and tried to smile, not really understanding the question.

"Yes," she decided was the safest answer, wondering if the man thought she might be planning to get up and start trouble.

"Well I never!" The man exclaimed from under his white moustache. "I've never heard such rudeness. Young lady, this seat is reserved for those who need to sit down. I'm old, I carry a stick. Do you have a problem? Are your young legs broken? You don't look like you're disabled!"

Sally knew about this. She remembered something from school about it, she just hadn't realized, much to her own embarrassment. They'd done a whole role play about this in drama class and she knew she should have offered the man her seat. But before she could jump up and apologize Amy stood up.

"Excuse me sir but I am her carer. Is there a problem?" She asked.

"She's sitting in the seat for the disabled," the man said, gesturing with his stick towards Sally.

"Yes, well, she is disabled!" Amy said smiling. "She has autism which means she can't understand things like money and where to sit and how to behave…"

The bus was slowing down ready to stop and Sally had two choices: hit her or run. She managed to count to twenty-three in her head then the bus stopped, the doors opened and she fled. She made it all the way home by herself by following the road signs she recognized. Amy was in quite a state when she too made it to Sally's house, in floods of tears and talking like she had a cold. Although Sally hated to see people upset she found it hard to feel too bad for her. She'd never felt as humiliated as she had done on that bus.

The result was that they said she was too high risk to be taken out anymore. And so she stayed in on Thursday's nights now and had to settle watching programs about others going out and having fun.

3

Jimmy, Robert and Aalap sat with Charlie, another friend, in their class's cornered off area of the local college's canteen. They each had a cheese and baked bean filled baked potato in front of them that their teacher had just gone to get. The canteen was like nothing they'd experienced before; the laughing, the shouting, the rough housing and most of all the swearing. Words were coming from all around them that they had only heard in films they'd watched without their parents knowing. A couple of times, when they'd been round Robert's house, they'd managed to sneak films out of his older brother's room and watch them on Robert's personal computer.

They were doing a taster session at the nearest mainstream college, even though most of them had been told they would probably need to go to a residential, special needs post nineteen provision to carry on their education once they left Hollygroves. They had been shown round the college first thing, then undergone taster lessons in woodwork and mechanics, but in neither lesson were they actually allowed to use any tools. Now, sat in the canteen, they took up six tables for the eight students, four teaching assistants and two teachers. Much to the displeasure of the eighty seven enrolled college pupils who were cramped up on the remaining eleven tables, shooting withering glances or muttering 'special' under their breath.

A couple of Jimmy's class mates were not happy, sitting with fingers in their ears and moaning or talking loudly to try and drown out some of the sound. Jimmy and his mates were thriving though. All four couldn't keep their eyes off the girls who marched around in short skirts and low cut tops, scowling when they noticed anyone looking; especially the boys who didn't have the social understanding to look away. Luckily they also didn't really understand what scowling meant. On top of that, the noise, the atmosphere, the electricity felt just like a college film or school drama that they all watched and all wanted to be part of. If they ignored the bright red rope which sectioned them off from the others, they could feel like they were part of a scene that was so... so appropriate. If only they could get past the barrier, then they wouldn't be the students with special needs anymore, they could just be students. They were glad Charlie was with them as he was generally regarded as the coolest kid in year nine, with his baggy trousers, smart t-shirts, earring like Beckham and long, straight hair. Both Jimmy and Aalap could also fit in easily. Robert was slightly more obvious with his rounded face and his thin eyes that came with his down syndrome, but otherwise they were all pretty cool with their fashionable jeans and t-shirts.

"You cats looking forward to holidays?" Charlie asked the guys as they tucked into their food.

"Yes cats," Aalap replied, his eyes moving along with a young lady queuing at the counter, "I am doing sports for autism activity cats. What are you doing?"

"Do they do wrestling?" Robert asked. "I am doing drama club, but they do not teach wrestling like The Undertaker."

"I am doing art club," Charlie said, "it is because I am very good at art you see and will one day sell my work and have a big house in America."

"I am doing my brother's party. And I am doing activity," Jimmy said. "Maybe it is the same activity as you Aalap. But I do not want to do sports."

"I do not know cats. I will ask and see if they do doing wrestling and other activities," Aalap said. "You are doing party?" He added with un-disguised envy.

"Yes," Jimmy said. "It will be a great party."

"Will there be girls there?" Robert asked.

"Yes," Jimmy told him.

"That's great, 'cos I love the laaaadiess!" Robert said, thumping the table.

"Yeah, how many girlfriends have you had?" Charlie asked. "I have had twenty seven girlfriends and I have done loads of kissing. The girls love *me*!"

"Yeah," said Robert less assured, "me too."

"Sure they do," Charlie said shaking his head slowly.

Just then laughter erupted from a nearby table of four young men and three girls. Jimmy, Charlie, Robert and Aalap looked over to them, while on the next table their classmate Ben, moaned louder and pushed his fingers deeper into his ears in response. Charlie tried to catch the attention of the table of students and when they didn't notice him, he started laughing as well. Soon enough Robert, Jimmy and Aalap were chuckling along, laughing first as loudly as the other table and then even louder. They were laughing so hard in fact that the other table noticed, stopped and turned round to look at them and the four lads didn't even notice.

It took a few minutes for them to notice the others had stopped laughing but when they did, they stopped as well,

"Bloody special needs," one of the young men from the other table snarled. Loud enough so Jimmy, Aalap, Robert and Charlie could hear, not so loud the teachers, who were engrossed in keeping the higher needs guys in the class calm, would hear.

Charlie got up and moved to Ben's table, leaving the stunned three to themselves. Unable to see anything funny anymore they turned nervously back to their food, finishing it in silence and as quickly as they could.

Later on, back at their own school, they sat at their desks while Mrs Gregory asked them about the day they had had and what they'd enjoyed the most.

"The art work," Helen said.

"Yes, and what else?" Mrs Gregory asked.

"The art work." Helen said, twisting her ribbons round and round her fingers.

"I am very good at art and am going to art club in holidays," Charlie piped up. "Some boys laughed at Jimmy, Robert and Aalap today."

"Oh, that wasn't nice of them. We just have to ignore them or come and tell me next time boys," She said to the embarrassed threesome.

"Okay and what about you Kirin?"

"Yeah!" Said Kirin, glancing at Mrs Gregory then turning back to his doodling on his books.

"Did you like it?" She asked

"Yeah!" Kirin said.

"Good," said Mrs Gregory, "Maybe we can look at that for you for when school finishes?"

"But Kirin always says yeah," Jimmy called from the back of the room. "How do you know he likes it?"

"Jimmy, enough," Mrs Gregory said, her cheeks turning a bit red. "You're being cheeky. Did you like the college Robert?"

"I did not see any wrestling classes. Where do I go to learn to do wrestling?" Robert asked.

"I don't know to be honest Robert. I don't know."

"Why was I being cheeky?" Jimmy asked.

"Because…because you were, okay? Now that's enough Jimmy or I'll be calling your mum."

"Okay," Jimmy said, head resting back on his hand as he stared down at the cracks in the wooden table.

"Right then. Well, I think that's enough for today guys. It's three O'clock so if you'd like to pack away your things into your trays and then go with Miss Fields, Mr Long and Mrs Samson to the car park where your buses and your Mums and Dads will be waiting."

In the car park Jimmy said goodbye to his best mates. Robert got into his Mum's car and Aalap got on the bus that went around the estate that he lived on. Jimmy had been round there only once; his mum had never let him go back. The house was fine, she had said, and the family lovely but the area spelt trouble with all those gangs of kids and the front door looked like it could be broken down easily. But then she didn't really like him going to Robert's house. Robert's oldest brother had been in prison before and this made Jimmy's mum really nervous, although Jimmy couldn't see why. He was never at home and he had only stolen a car, it wasn't like he was dangerous. Sometimes people in the films Jimmy watched stole cars and they were okay. And Jimmy didn't even have a car, so couldn't understand the problem.

Jimmy wished he could go out more; see his friends more like his older brother Tim and younger brother Sam got to do. He understood that he was different and needed some help with writing, spelling, money and a few other bits, but he knew that he could do other things. Seeing the guys at college today had made Jimmy think. The whole way back on the bus he sat with his head pressed up against the window, his eyes shut trying to figure out what it was that made him so different from them. Different so he always had to have an adult around and he always had to have set rules and have his hand held. He decided then that he'd find out when he got back in.

At home he took his snack and juice up to the study on the second floor. The one that his Dad used to write emails or do research for his company. Jimmy wasn't allowed in there for very long, his mum was nervous around the already heavily fire-walled and child protected internet.

"What do you want to do up there?" His mum had said when he'd asked, surprised he didn't just want to put films on like he normally did.

"I want to do looking at facebook and I want to do looking at films," Jimmy said, omitting rather then lying, unsure how his mum would react.

"Okay. But Tim needs the computer for his college course-work, so you'll have to let him use it when he gets home."

"Okay," Jimmy had said.

The first obstacle he came across was the spelling of Autism, but he had seen the word before and noticed it written across many of the books on the white shelves around the large study, so he picked one out and copied the word from the spine into the search engine that came up by default. He pressed enter and started to scan his way down the thousands of results.

Most of the results were journal articles and Jimmy opened up a couple in new windows so he could go back to the results, should he need to. Jimmy could read okay, his reading age was nine, but he couldn't understand these journals. They said things like:

Autism is a developmental and neurological dis-order that is characterized by an impaired social understanding and repetitive behavior.

This didn't explain why he needed his hand held or why he had to sit in a separate section of a canteen or why people shook their heads when he said he wanted to work in films.

Others said things like:

People with autism engage in strange and different behavioral patterns, People with autism benefit from sensory and visual learning.

Frustrated, Jimmy kept on clicking down, through websites and web links like *'Your autistic child.' 'How to treat Autism.' 'Scholarly articles on ASD,'* and the like, but he couldn't find any that he understood.

In the end he even tried flicking through some of the books, but these didn't help either. What was an Autistic spectrum? What is Pathological non-avoidance? Or Pervasive developmental disorder? Nothing seemed to tell him anything.

But if he could find out what it all meant then maybe he could begin to fit in better? Maybe if he knew why he had to sit one side of that red rope in the canteen, then he could move over to the other side?

He decided right then that that would be his project. He decided he would find out what Autism meant. Then maybe he wouldn't mind so much when someone held his hand.

4

Sally was sitting on the old, tattered sofa that had been placed facing the clubhouse entrance, on her own. She wrote mostly nonsensical texts on her mobile phone that she wasn't going to send, merely saving them as drafts which she'd later read. She hoped from the outside she looked like the teenagers she saw on their phones at bus stops or walking along the streets.

Around her lots of young people played, aged between fourteen and nineteen and occupying themselves in different ways. One handsome seventeen year old man, whom Sally had met many times before, was fascinated by these plastic, red, building bricks and he sat cross legged in front of one of the walls with its yellowing wall paper and was throwing the bricks up against the wall and laughing as they fell. He always looked so happy, Sally thought. So happy that she had tried this at home once, but hadn't got the same buzz that he seemed to get.

Another young person, a girl of about fifteen, was play-ing with ribbons, holding them out and wiggling them so they danced and played in front of her. Sally had known her from these groups for two years now and every summer was the same, she'd turn up with her ribbons and just want to play with them, getting upset when she couldn't, when support staff took them away.

At a small, old pool table with flaps of torn felt and one leg shorter then the other, were two young men. They were chatting and laughing with one another. They high-fived when they got a ball in then chased it across the laminate tiled floor when it fell through the nets which were supposed to cover the pockets. Sally used to spend time with these two, until Bob and her became something of an item. This hadn't lasted long and things had been somewhat awkward since they'd broken up last summer. Sally had been looking for something a bit more serious but Bob and his mum had stopped it all when Sally had made a habit of phoning the house phone nine times a day, including once at three thirty on a Sunday morning. Now they didn't talk and once again Sally was on her own.

Around the playing teenagers milled staff members wearing bright yellow t-shits, holding steaming cups of tea, talking and flirting with each other. Occasionally they interacted with the young people when the group leader came out from the kitchen with her folder and clip board to check everything was still running smooth.

"We'll give ten more minutes for late comers," the group leader said loudly towards the crowds. "Then we'll head into town." Sally looked up at her, tried to catch her eye and smile, but Mel was too busy these days. She had to organize whole groups of young people, not like when it had just been the two of them.

Sally looked upwards as the doorbell went again. Mel re-emerged and headed to the first set of locked doors that she opened by punching in a code.

Two, five, eight, two, Sally rattled off in her mind as she watched. She could pick up codes like that easily; it had been a cause of problems at school before. She watched Mel disappear through that set of doors and heard her punch in the next code, *(one four seven, one)* to let more people through the entrance.

A few moments later and a young man came in with his Mum, both of whom Sally didn't recognize. The Mum was talking loudly at Mel who was nodding along and smiling, only half listening. The young man was handsome, with his hair he'd gelled up at the front and his checkered shirt that he wore over the top of a black t-shirt.

"Now, you understand he needs support on buses all the time. He's not like other young men, you know? You'll need to watch him all the time, hold his hand across the roads?" The young man's mum was saying.

"Of course, yep, no problem," Mel said, distracted now by Danielle who was making a mess of the ball pool, throwing balls out against the wall where they rebounded and landed all around creating tripping hazards. "Gem, can you sort that?" She said to one of the care workers, who smiled and tore herself away from her conversation to go and coax Danielle out of the pool.

"…And you understand he needs count downs and plenty of warning of change?" The mum continued, much to the obvious embarrassment of the young man she was with.

"Of course, no trouble," Mel said. "Jimmy, would you like to meet some people?"

29

"Yes, I…" Jimmy started.

"Now, he doesn't make friends easily," the mum said. "It's because of his autism, you understand? These people like to be on their own, doing their own thing. You can introduce him to people, but you have to know, he'll get on better with the adults 'cos they're more patient and can use all the different tools."

"Well, we'll see how it goes," Mel said, distracted now by the sound of a car pulling up in the car park outside. "Jimmy, would you like to meet my friend Sally?" She said, looking towards the sofa by the entrance, using the Makaton sign language as she addressed him straight for the first time.

"Sure, sounds good," Jimmy said, in a quiet voice that Sally thought was sweet. The group of three then moved towards the sofa, where Sally was still pretending to text, the mum looking around the whole time wringing her hands, the young man a pace in front of her.

"Sally, this is my friend Jimmy," Mel said to Sally, still signing even though she knew Sally could understand without it. "Jimmy, this is Sally. Would you like to sit beside her?"

Just then the doorbell went again and she was off, with quick apologies, to answer it.

"Hi Sally," the mum said as Jimmy took a seat on Sally's right, draping his arm over the arm rest. He pushed himself close to it so him and Sally were as far away from each other as they could have been. "I'm Mrs Tiffin and this is my son, Jimmy. How old are you?"

"I'm fifteen years old. My birthday is the 23rd of June," Sally replied, still not looking up.

"Oh, there you are Jimmy. Same age as you."

"No, my birthday is the 25th of August and I am fourteen," Jimmy said.

"Which school do you go to?" Sally asked Jimmy quickly before his mum got another word in.

"He goes to Hollygroves, don't you Jimmy? What school do you go to?" Mrs Tiffin said, leaving Jimmy's mouth hanging half open.

"Glen Park."

"Well, that sounds lovely. We looked at that school, didn't we Jimmy? But we decided you needed somewhere with a bit more support, so we went with Hollygroves." Mrs Tiffin was smiling a little too broadly, still wringing her hands as the conversation lapsed into silence. The silence then grew thick as all three watched Mel sign in another young person. The mum at the door simply signed him in and walked out and Sally could see that Jimmy wished his mum would do the same.

Eventually, Mrs Tiffin stood.

"Well, I suppose I'll get going now," she said, eyes darting about the room. "Can I go?" She asked a nearby support worker.

"Sure, no trouble," the support worker told her.

"Will you keep an eye on My Jimmy?" She asked him, motioning towards the sofa.

"Course, will do," the support worker, a young man in his late teens with spots and glasses said. He moved and sat himself on the arm rest. "Hey bud, I'm Carl. Nice to meet you." He extended a hand which Jimmy took lightly and shook.

"Okay then," Mrs Tiffin said, leaning over to Jimmy and kissing his cheek. "I'll see you back here at four O'clock. Have a great time bowling, get a strike for me!"

She smiled again, awkwardly hovering for a moment before finally starting a slow walk towards the exit.

"So, you like bowling bud?" Carl said to Jimmy.

"Yeah, it is good. I go sometimes with Dad or School. Why do you call me bud?"

"It's short for buddy, or friend," Carl said.

"But it's part of a flower," Jimmy said.

"True, true," Carl said looking away, up and down the room.

"Do you like school?" Sally said turning now to Jimmy, catching his eye in hers briefly, before both flinched away.

"School's okay. I like some bits. I like project and art and sometimes activity. But not all the time. I like Robert and Aalap as well. Do they come to club?"

Sally shook her head.

"No."

"Oh," Jimmy said. "Do you like school?"

Sally shook her head again.

"I like cooking and café and project. But I hate Mr Beedle."

"Do you know the film 'Ice Age Three' about Buck who says, 'he's the one who gave me this' when he points to his eye?" Jimmy said, having watched the film that morning at home.

"I like that film. My favorite film is Gladiator. Do you like Gladiator?" Sally asked, watching as Carl stood from the sofa arm and moved back towards the kitchen. "It's about a man who's a gladiator and he cuts this person's head off and he says 'are you entertained?"

"Don't like that," Jimmy said. "It's wrong."

"Why wrong?"

"When he cuts his head off at first his sword's in one hand, then the other hand, then his other. It's wrong."

"Why does it do that?"

"Dunno," Jimmy said, shrugging.

"Right guys! We all ready to go?" Mel interjected from the kitchen doorway, interrupting the conversation both Jimmy and Sally had been beginning to enjoy. "Come on guys, let's get moving."

The group traveled in two mini buses. Sally and Jimmy sat side by side in the first one, comfortable already, conversation flowing if not quite smooth as water, more like sand or gravel. On the bus they were one of only three pairs chatting. Other young people had brought their toys with them and were playing loudly and noisily, something Sally was used to on these groups and Jimmy was used to at school. Each young person there was happy doing their thing, playing their game. Often Jimmy found himself envying them, though wasn't sure why. Maybe because they seemed so happy, so free to do what they wanted and they didn't find social situations hard like him.

But Jimmy was glad he'd met Sally, someone to talk to and be with. It made him not mind so much that Robert and Aalap weren't there.

At the bowling alley they made sure they were on the same lane together. Jimmy counted fourteen young people and twelve staff members in those yellow t-shirts. Together they took up three lanes; the young people bowling, the staff drinking coffee or reluctantly sitting with their assigned one to one. Because of the picture his mum had painted Jimmy had been allocated a one to one support worker, a lady called Ezie with a heavy accent Jimmy couldn't place. She would hover around him or sit next to him, repeatedly asking if he was okay and whether he needed the bumpers up. She went with him to buy a coke, even though he was perfectly capable. She even paid for it with his money then left her hand waiting for the change which she handed back to him, watching as he slipped it into the zippered compartment of his wallet.

It seemed to Jimmy like his turn kept coming around too often. He didn't mind bowling, he was pretty good at it, but this morning he was happy sitting in those linked plastic chairs, watching the screen or talking to Sally.

"What do you want to do when you leave school?" He asked her, thinking back to that meeting three weeks ago that had led him to these activity groups.

"School doesn't start until September," She answered, shooting him a quizzical look.

"No, when school ends completely. Like going to do work."

"I don't know to be honest," Sally replied.

"Oh."

"How do you know what to do for work?"

"You do something that you are good at and have learned about."

"Well. Maybe I'd do cooking. I'm good at cooking. I do cooking at home for my mum and for me. I make sandwiches and pasta and do chopping of vegetables to put in sauces."

"I don't know if I can do cooking because I have autism," Jimmy said. "My mum won't let me use knives to do chopping."

"Oh. But I also... never mind," Sally said, looking around her.

"Okay," said Jimmy, now watching the staff try to persuade a young man he'd been introduced to as Ed, leave his red building blocks behind to push the ball down the ramp. Ed was making quite a bit of noise now, much to the obvious irritation of a group of teenagers on the lane next to them.

"I am going to do partying on Thursday," Jimmy said. It would be the first time he had ever been allowed to stay up for one of Tim's parties.

"Okay. I do a lot of partying," Sally said a bit too quickly.

"Oh. Okay," Jimmy said, feeling the same pangs of jealously that Aalap and Robert had felt when he'd mentioned the party at the college outing a few days before.

"Yes. It is good," Sally lied as they both turned to watch Ed push one of the support workers away and try and get back to his seat where more of his blocks were. "I talk to people and sometimes things break but I dance and... and other party things like that."

"Need to go to the toilet," Jimmy said, all of a sudden, feeling the tightness in his gut again.

"You go to the toilet a lot," Sally stated as Jimmy rose. Jimmy slung his bag over his shoulder and moved down the pattern flooring shadowed by Ezie.

Once inside a locked cubical Jimmy sat down on the closed lid and put his bag on his lap. He then opened the zip of his Reebok rucksack and fished out three things; a film case for the Matrix Two, the letter that had invited him to the group and a piece of lined paper with a homemade schedule of the day written on to it, derived from the letter that had told him what the plans would be. Jimmy knew that people wouldn't have minded him looking these over in front of them. Many of the other young people had schedules they carried with them, made from little pictures with words. But the thing was he'd been really looking forward to this day since the letter had come, mostly because of his older brother Tim.

Back when he was eleven, twelve, thirteen he'd watch as Tim's friends came round when Tim was thirteen, fourteen, fifteen and now sixteen and they went out together to the cinema or to each other's houses or to the bowling ally. Jimmy felt stabs of envy each time as he anticipated an evening in with his parents and later his films. So when he got to thirteen, he'd asked his mum if he could go and walk to Aalap's house, just twenty minutes down the road but his Mum had said no.

But now, finally, after four years stuck at home or on day trips with his parents; *here he was*, bowling with people his age, just like his brother had done. Just like every teenager did, Jimmy assumed, apart from him. But the point was, those people, they never had schedules or PEC's symbols with them or adults wearing yellow t-shirts. And although Jimmy knew there was nothing he could do about the adults, or his shadow, he'd be damned if he'd let anyone see his schedule; damned if people were going to know that he, if not needed it, felt a hell of a lot better just looking at it, knowing what was to happen next. So after four minutes of scanning his eyes down the page, he got up, remembering to flush, then packed away his bits and walked back outside to the slight relief of Ezie.

Back at the lanes it was his turn already and the others had been growing a bit impatient. Jimmy quickly chose a nice, smooth, blue ball and carried it up to the line before throwing it, straight as he could, towards the pins. The ball hit the bumpers and bounced twice before hitting the furthest pin on the right and knocking it down flat, along with two others, to the rippling applause of the late twenties staff coupled with a: 'get in, nice shot Jim.' He smiled to himself, but then made the mistake of glancing left just as one of the teenagers in the next lane got a strike, to the cheers of his mates.

Frustrated, Jimmy went back and chose a yellow, heavier ball, and continued to knock over a further four pins, to further scattered applause.

"Nice one mate," a male staff member said as he passed, raising his hand for a high five which Jimmy reluctantly gave.

The day drew to an end, all too quickly for both Sally and Jimmy who'd been more than happy sitting together, talking and letting the others mill around their peripheries. As they sat on the bus, Jimmy wanted to ask more questions, but for some reason these wouldn't or couldn't come out.

"Sally?" He asked her,

"Yes?" She answered. "Why has your voice gone croaky?"

"Don't know," he said looking away.

"What is wrong?" She asked her voice softer now.

"Do you have facebook?"

"I have facebook. I have fifty two friends."

"Do you think if I added you would accept me?" Jimmy asked, his stomach now swirling a little.

"Yes," Sally said, before reaching down into her purse to find some paper and a pen. "This is my name. Search for me then add me as a friend and I will accept it. I really only have nineteen friends, I just forgot."

Jimmy took the paper from her hand and as he did, brushed her skin just slightly, feeling his heart beat quicken like it did when Neo and Trinity see each other again at the beginning of the Matrix two. He wasn't sure why he had been so worried, he had many friends on facebook too, but he needed to be able to talk to her and next week seemed so far away.

"Okay," he said, putting the paper in the breast pocket of his shirt.

On the same sofa on which they'd met that morning, Jimmy and Sally sat, waiting and watching for parents to arrive.

"What will you do when you get home?" Jimmy asked.

"I will have dinner and then I will go to art club and then I will go home and watch TV," Sally said.

"I will watch films then have dinner," Jimmy said.

"Are you coming to activities next week?"

"Yes. Every Tuesday I will be doing activity."

Just then the door bell rang and they both watched as Mel glanced at her watch, before walking swiftly to the door;

her large red file perched under one arm, papers poking out precariously.

Jimmy was both un-surprised and disappointed to see his Mum walking behind Mel as she returned. His mum saw Jimmy sitting with Sally and her lips formed a lopsided kind of grin.

"Just where I left you both. Isn't it great that even with Autism these two have been sitting together. Have they been talking or is it just because they feel safe on the familiar sofa?"

"They've been chatting all day," Mel said.

"Oh. Okay, that's quite strange. Good though," Jimmy's mum frowned.

"Yep, think they've become pretty good friends."

"Jimmy!" His mum called to him now, taking a step closer to him. "How was your day?"

"Good. Bowling was good. This is Sally. She is my friend. Why is it strange?"

"Of course she is sweet heart. You ready to go home?"

"Hi Mrs Tiffin," said Sally, "how was your day?"

"Good thank you Sally," Jimmy's mum replied "I'm glad you two got on, thank you for looking after my Jimmy. You ready to go Jim?"

"You can wait?" Sally said.

"No, thank you Sally but we have to go. Thank you Mel for the day. Do we need to sign out?"

"No, that's okay, I've seen he's safe."

"Okay then. Let's go," She said, taking Jimmy's hand and half pulling him to his feet.

"Bye Sally," Jimmy said quietly, turning back towards her as he left.

"Bye Jimmy. See you next activity," Sally called after him. .

Sally was still sat there ten minutes after everyone else had gone, when her Mum turned up.

"Sorry I'm late," Sally's mum said with no real feeling behind the words. "Lost track of time."

"That's okay Helen. Just please try and remember for next time," Mel replied.

"I'll be here four O'clock sharp next week," she said, pulling Sally to her, putting an uncomfortable arm around her shoulders that Sally tried to avoid but couldn't. She hated being pulled in to her mum's bosom that reeked of smoke.

Out in the car park Helen got into the driver's side and reached across to undo the passenger's side lock. Sally opened the door then removed the take away packages, cigarette packets and empty coke cans that covered the seat, placing them in the back before climbing in and clicking her seat belt on. The car smelt stale as it always did, but Sally didn't want to start an argument by rolling down the window.

"Good time?" her mum asked her.

"Yes."

"What did you do?" She asked, pulling out the electronic gates of the car park, shifting the gears loudly.

"Bowling and chatting."

"Yeah?"

"Yeah. I met a boy. He's very nice," Sally said, looking over to her mum who snorted quietly and kept staring at the road ahead.

Sally felt her muscles tense and her temper rise. She caught it though, she caught it just like she'd been taught and focused all her energy out the window, picturing the next road sign along the familiar route and reading them in her head as she passed.

Helen dropped Sally off, hung her keys on the little hook next to the door, picked up her coat and was off to meet her friends.

Sally made herself quick poached eggs on toast, showered, changed and then waited for the bus to come and pick her up for art club.

Sally went to all the clubs she could. This was mostly because her mum and her didn't get on very well so every time their social worker suggested something, they jumped at it. It was also because Sally got to do these things for free as her mum hadn't worked ever since her dad left. She enjoyed some of the clubs and tolerated the rest, but she was happy being out the house, especially over the holidays when there was less escape from each other.

The mini bus picked her up at ten past six. James and Eve came and knocked for her together and gave her the prepared note and mini-lecture when her mum wasn't there to sign her off again.

The bus was already half full and was the same company that had provided the bus for the social services activity earlier. Looking around at the empty spaces left Sally found herself wishing that Jimmy was sitting near the back saving a seat for her.

He wasn't like the other guys she met, who were few and far between anyhow; he seemed different, sweeter and easier to talk to. She hadn't felt disabled when she spoke with him and that was so rare for her. She wanted to talk about him, wished her mum would have asked, but she wasn't going to be doing that anytime soon.

The art club was held in a church hall and was run by a charity rather then the local government. There was a larger age range here; club members were between twelve and twenty five and most were already concentrating on drawing, painting or sticking together bits of construction paper by the time she walked in. Only one person looked up to greet her:

"Hi Sally," Charlie said as she walked into the hall.

"Hi Charlie," she replied going over to the table he was sitting at.

"How are you sweet heart?" He asked, getting up and giving her a hug.

"I am okay," Sally replied, cheeks flushing crimson. She broke from the hug as quick as she could. He was handsome and charming, she'd give him that, but she'd gone down that road with him before and it wasn't something she would do again. Occasionally she'd slip up and when her esteem was particularly low she'd let him hold her hand and even kiss her if a staff member turned their back for fifteen seconds, but today she was feeling too good.

"How is your girlfriend?" She asked.

"Emma is not at club today," Charlie replied giving her a wink. "So I can hang around with you sweetheart."

"But I do not think Emma would like that."

"Yes, but Emma is not here. Maybe we can do kissing later?"

"I don't think my boyfriend would like that," Sally said grinning, though not certain where the fib came from.

"You have a boyfriend now?" Charlie asked, temper rising just noticeably which made Sally smile even more.

"Yes. His name is Jimmy Tiffin," She replied quickly. "He is very handsome and knows a lot about films."

"Jimmy Tiffin goes to my school!" Charlie said. "I am better at art then he is and art is the best the teacher said so."

"Jimmy goes to your school?" Sally asked, feeling herself go a bit cold. "You can not tell him I said that he was my boyfriend!"

"Why?"

"You are not allowed to!" Sally said, before turning sharply and walking down the hall to where the crafts table was, concerned now that Jimmy would find out what she said and not want to talk to her. She fiddled for a while with some green felt and some pipe cleaners before wandering over to the computers where she normally spent most of her time. She wasn't really supposed to use the internet but staff normally just let her, knowing by now how little she really liked art.

The first thing she did was check her Facebook. And sure enough, there it was in the corner, that little + symbol with 'one friend request' by it. Sally clicked on the icon and up popped a picture of Jimmy standing in what she presumed was his bedroom, smiling up at the camera. She confirmed the request then went straight to his wall to write:

Hello Jimmy.

I will see you at the next activity. Have a good week.

Sally,
X

P.S. I have not told people you are my boyfriend.

And then pressed send.

5

Jimmy replied to the post two days later whilst his Mum, Dad and younger brother were setting up for Tim's 17th birthday party. Tim was upstairs in his room, creating CDs with a couple of his mates whilst the others did the brunt of the work:

Hello Sally.

He had written, but wasn't sure what else to put. He wasn't planning on telling anyone that Sally was his girlfriend, he knew they had to talk about it before he could. But he had not been able to stop thinking about her for the last two days; the way she smiled, the way she laughed, the way she always brushed her hair back behind her ears. He stared at her message again. What should he write? He wanted to let her how well they had got on, how nice it was to talk to someone non-stop like that with no awkwardness. How much he just wanted to see her and how pretty he thought she was because that was a compliment you could say to anyone, even if they only wanted to be friends. For fifteen minutes he thought about this, until he finally wrote:

Hello Sally.

See you at group next week.

I have not told anyone you are my girlfriend.

Jimmy, x

Then signed out of his account.

The message sent he wandered out into their garden where a large, green and white striped gazebo was set up over their large 'crazy paved' patio, which had already lost the potted plants and the hanging baskets his mum prized.

"Here Jimmy, do these will you?" His mum asked, handing him a packet of multi-colored balloons and a hand pump.

He took them from her and tore the packet open with his teeth. He'd done this a few times before so needed no instructions. He went and sat down on one of their dining room chairs that were doubling up as party seating around the edge of the Gazebo.

He started pumping the balloons, watching as they filled but needing to pass them to his Dad to tie when they were full to nearly bursting. His dad was draping colored lights around the edges, moving the stepladder about so he could tie them to the Gazebo's metal skeleton. He didn't seem to mind the quick interruptions as Jimmy passed more and more to him, until the floor was covered with red, yellow, green and blue balloons which combined with the soft lighting already shining from disco lights above, created a shimmering effect which made Jimmy's excitement bubble.

Tim had parties for his birthday most years but for the last two Jimmy had, had to stay in his room. Now he was going to be allowed to join in even though there would be alcohol around and plenty of it. His mum had, among the list of instructions she had rattled off to Tim, even mentioned allowing him a beer which would be his first.

"Now, you just make sure he goes upstairs before 9:30," she had said to Tim earlier. "Any later and… and you'll be in trouble," she had added.

Tim smiled at this. She was going to say any later and there'd be too many drunk people, dancing and smoking, but she didn't want to admit that him and his friends did anything of the sort.

"Of course mum," he said winking at Jimmy.

Tim probably understood Jimmy the best in his family. He had grown up thinking his mum was strict on him, not letting him out past eight on a weekday, even when he was sixteen. Going crazy when he got caught smoking at school, picking him up ten-thirty sharp from parties. But after seeing the way she was with Jimmy, he realized how lucky he had had it. Tonight he was determined to make sure his little brother had a good time.

"I'm relying on you and your friends to look out for him. Anything happens, I'll be blaming you."

"Yes mum," Tim said.

"You know I'm trusting you here."

"Yes mum."

"Just be careful."

"Yes mum."

The picnic table was covered with plates of sandwiches that would go untouched, crisps that would quickly diminish and bottles of beer that would need to be constantly replenished from the Tiffin's meager supplies and from what people brought. Music was pouring now out of the stereo. The neighbors, despite the warning, shut windows and patio doors with poignant bangs that reverberated in the otherwise quiet suburban evening.

Tim's friends started arriving at 7pm. His best friends from college came first, weighted down with carrier bags full of brightly colored alcho-pops and warm cans of cheap lager. Jimmy had retreated to his room some time before, which faced onto the garden and the gazebo. He had opened his windows so he could listen as people arrived before he took the plunge and joined in. His parents had also gone to their room, still trying to gently convince each other they were doing the right thing. They re-assured each other that if the people downstairs weren't drinking in their garden then they'd just have gone to a colder and rather more dangerous public park or hung around town trying to get into pubs and clubs. Only Sam, Jimmy's younger brother, stayed downstairs with Tim, trying to entrain the steadily growing number of guests who patiently watched his haphazard break dancing as they drank, sitting in chairs; waiting for the self confidence to get up and dance or to talk to the girl they'd had a crush on for some time, all watching the door as different people arrived.

Up in his room Jimmy had put a film on through his Playstation that was connected to the small television set his parents had reluctantly given him one Christmas. He watched Die Hard for the twenty seventh and a half time, mumbling the words under his breath as he did, hoping the volume was loud enough for the people downstairs to hear the gun fire and explosions. *This will make them know I'm cool,* he thought to himself. *This'll impress them.* He had picked this film for two reasons. The first was the street cred that he knew came attached to this film. He had heard not only his brother and his friends rave about this one, but plenty of the teaching assistants at school as well and they were cool, they went out all the time. The second reason was for its one hundred and thirty one minute run time. Two hours and eleven minutes from when he's gone up at six. Eleven minutes past eight. At eleven minutes past eight he would go downstairs and socialize. A respectable hour and eleven minutes after the party officially started. He could then have his beer, maybe dance a little, talk a little and most importantly; fit in.

But as his film was drawing to a close, only twelve minutes left, he began to get a knot in his throat. Below him he could hear the voices getting louder, the laughter getting longer and deeper from the guys, shriller from the girls, the conversation moving swiftly from soft whispers that only just carried to him, to loud shouts and exited giggles.

When the film ended and the credits began, he got himself up and went into the bathroom where he checked himself over in the full length mirror that hung against the yellow, floral wallpaper his parents had recently put up. He was wearing his favorite jeans that were a faded brown along with a green t-shirt with Ben Sherman written upon it, a hand-me-down from Tim some months ago. He wet his hands under the, ornate, silver taps, then ran his hands through his hair, before picking up his brother's deodorant can and coating his clothes in it. He was ready, he thought, as he'd ever be.

The trip downstairs took him no time at all, he felt almost like he was flying down the last few steps, fighting an insatiable urge to do a u-turn and go watch the other die hard under his X-men duvet. But he didn't, steeling himself he walked on. His heart beat quickened, but not so much as it had when Sally had given him that slip of paper with her name on it and said that he could look her up. He wished that she was here sharing in this, they could have got though it together.

From the bottom of the stairs he could see into the kitchen where two boys were filling his mum's plastic cake mix bowl with a combination of different spirits and soft drinks. One of them noticed and looked up, smiled and waved Jimmy over. He was James who Jimmy had met a few times before. He often came and picked Tim up to drive him to college and sometimes he came round in the evenings to watch films or play computer games with Tim in his room.

"Jimmy me ole mucker," he said, "come over here and try some of this. It'll put hairs on your chest."

"I'm only allowed one beer," Jimmy said towards the floor.

"Well, this isn't beer eh?" James said with a wink. Jimmy quickly scanned through the memories in his head of where he had seen winks before. He knew that could mean a lot of things and could only think of one.

"Are you joking with me?" He asked.

"No mate," James said, catching his friend's eye and sharing a smile. "Do you like coke? And pineapple juice?"

"Yes," Jimmy told him.

"Then you'll like this. That's pretty much all you can taste."

Jimmy moved to join them as James dunked a plastic cup into the brown-orange, carbonated concoction and pulled it out, three quarters full.

"Here," he said passing it to Jimmy who took it hesitantly.

"Thank you," he said raising the cup towards his lips.

"Hold on mate, hold on," James said, filling another cup for his friend then one for himself. "Let's do this right. What you have to do is hit each other's cups, gently, and say cheers. Ready?"

"Okay."

"Right. Cheers!" James said raising his cup and knocking it into Jimmy's.

"Cheers," Jimmy said, doing the same, first to James' cup then to the other guy's.

"Cheers!" The other guy said.

They all took sips. They were right; it just tasted of coke and pineapple juice, a strange mix and one that didn't taste all that nice, but then the others were drinking it so Jimmy just assumed that was what was done at parties.

Feeling more confident with a drink in his hand, Jimmy stepped out the sliding patio doors into the main part of the party which was nearly full now; people were spilling out the gazebo into the garden. Lots of people were smoking which made Jimmy recoil slightly, as he brushed past them, looking for Tim or for Sam.

Tim was by the CD-player and he began to make his way through the crowded space towards him.

"Jimmy!" Shouted a girl's voice as he passed. Jimmy turned to look, surprised someone recognized him, and found the girl, who was smiling and waving. She wore a low cut top and short skirt, she was a girl he had known for a while but who looked different now not on her way to college. "Give me a hug," she said moving from her group of friends and pulling him to her. "This is Tim's brother Jimmy," she said to the three boys that had been talking to her.

"Hello mate," one said, giving Jimmy a pat on the back. "How's it hanging?"

Jimmy was unsure what this meant, so decided to play it safe as he could.

"Have you seen Die Hard? It's about a man in a building who says Yipppe Ki Yay and has to put a dead person in a chair and put him in a lift and make the bad guys see him."

"Okay. How much of that stuff you had?" One of the guys asked, his brow furrowed, nodding in the direction of Jimmy's cup.

"Three sips. How much of that have you had?" Jimmy said, nodding towards the guy's beer can.

"It's okay, Jimmy is Autistic," the girl who he knew as Jill said, giving Jimmy a knowing smile. The words, although said in what she hoped was kindness, felt loaded to Jimmy and he felt small and somewhat deflated. He had thought he was doing so well so far.

"Are you!" One of the lads with a small goatee exclaimed. "Quick, you see the garden? How many blades of grass. Go!"

"I don't know," said Jimmy looking at the lawn confused.

"You don't? I thought you people could do all sorts of tricks? What was the day of the week on… the twenty second of April in 1932?"

"I don't know," said Jimmy, even quieter this time.

"Hello little brother," Tim said suddenly appearing, having seen Jimmy come out into the garden. "I see you've met some of my friends."

"Yes," said Jimmy, taking a longer sip of his drink.

"Good, hope they're being good. You got yourself some punch? Well, they didn't say anything about that, eh?"

"No. They said I could have one beer."

"Well, just go careful, eh?" Tim said, taking a gulp of his own beer and lighting up a Marlboro, the first Jimmy had ever seen him smoke.

"What's go careful?"

"It means don't drink too much."

"Okay. What is too much?"

"Um… you'll know you've done too much when you get dizzy and feel ill."

"Okay," said Jimmy, "I will drink until I feel dizzy!"

"That's the spirit!" Jill said. "Let's all drink until we get dizzy!"

"Right then Jim," Tim said, "I just gotta pop over and see someone. You come find me if you need me and make sure everyone's good."

"Okay."

"Okay. I'll see you in a minute," Tim said and with that he wandered off, heading towards a tight circle of his mates who were standing just beyond the marquee, passing round what Jimmy assumed was a rather large cigarette.

Jimmy headed to the kitchen chairs that had been arranged around the edges to create a makeshift dance floor. Here he felt safer, the people next to him weren't talking, laughing or dancing. They too were sipping quickly from their plastic cup and when they had finished, they would get up, move around the growing numbers on the dance floor and go into the kitchen. Then after a minute or two they'd come back with their filled drinks. When Jimmy's cup was empty, he kept hold of it in his hands, cupping in protectively, waiting. As soon as one of other others had finished their drinks, he got up to follow. Looking ahead at the now packed tent and the gauntlet that this trip would prove to be, Jimmy felt his heart jump into his mouth and his head begin to ache.

Be like James Bond.

He whispered to himself.

Follow the bad man through the people and into the kitchen.

So he did. When the man in front of him disappeared into the throng, he made sure he kept up, always keeping an eye out for the man's red shirt and that made the whole thing easier. He didn't mind needing to push past people so much, or even ask them to step to one side so that he could get past. After all, James bond would never say 'excuse me' if he was chasing someone.

Five drinks later and Jimmy was dancing. Quite unsure how he'd made the transition from outsider to one of the lads, but here he was jumping up and down in a small circle with Tim, James, Gill and some others, not thinking so much, not worrying so much. He was enjoying himself, throwing himself around the garden like the others were doing, laughing at, but not really understanding the jokes that the others were shouting out over the music. He felt much freer somehow, the drinks having dampened and quieted those constant, worried thoughts.

When he went inside to get another drink, he saw that the kitchen was empty save for Jill who looked like she'd been crying.

Jimmy looked up at her and they had eye contact, then he put his cup into the bowl that had been recently replenished and for some reason had grapes, pens and a little wooden figure from his living room bouncing about in.

"You okay Jimmy?" She asked him,

"Yes," he said. "Are you okay?"

"No. My boyfriend just texted me, he didn't want me to go out tonight. Now he says he's going round to his ex's house. I hate him Jimmy, I hate him. I mean, I wasn't going to miss out on your brothers party because *my* ex was here, I've known your brother for years."

"Okay," Jimmy said, not really knowing what else to say.

"Thanks Jim, you're sweet. And cute too. Do you have a girlfriend?"

"I don't think so," said Jimmy. "I met a girl who is very nice and kind and pretty but she is not telling people I am her boyfriend."

"Aw, you poor thing. Come here," she said, taking Jimmy's hand. She gave him a hug then pulled back her head and kissed him on the lips. It was his first kiss, as she'd rightly assumed and Jimmy knew this was a big moment. It wasn't what he'd expected seeing the films, though it was nice enough, colder then he'd thought and she tasted sweet but smoky. Either way, a few seconds later when it was over he was glad it had happened.

"You're a good lad," Jill said smiling at the young man.

"Thank you," Jimmy said.

"Come on, let's go and dance."

Half an hour later and Tim was helping him to bed. He'd been watching Jimmy for some time and had been happy to see his brother enjoying himself so much. But he knew the party was over for him when he slipped over on the dance floor and went head first into the grass, to the laughter of all those around him and to Tim's surprise and respect, to Jimmy's amusement too.

It was half ten and his Mum and Dad were probably listening out. But they wouldn't give them a hard time now and Tim could put up with it all tomorrow. So what was a week of no lifts? It had been worth it.

"Was I okay? Did I do good partying?" Jimmy asked Tim as he led him up the stairs.

"You were brilliant little brother," Tim said to him,

"Yeah? Did I do good dancing?" Jimmy said as they got through the bedroom door and Tim sat him down on the bed.

"You did great dancing mate," Tim said.

"Good," Jimmy said, already drifting towards a deep and un-troubled sleep. He knew if his parents had heard any of that, he was going to be in more trouble then he had ever been before. But he didn't care.

"Tim?" He asked as his brother started tip-toeing out of the room. "Do you know what Autism is and why I need to have my hand held at school?"

"No mate, I don't really understand. I do know I think you're a star though. And don't think we didn't notice you kissing Jill in the kitchen you lucky man!"

"Oh. Okay," Jimmy said, straying further into sleep.

"Love you little brother," Tim said shutting the door.

"I love you too. Thank you for the partying," Jimmy said, finally drifting off as he spoke and the door was closed.

It had been the best night of his life so far.

6

Sally got woken up every morning at seven, first by Sammy the cat sitting on her chest and licking her cheeks, then ten minutes later by her alarm. Normally getting up was one of the things Sally hated most, but today she let her eyes spring open and she sat straight up, surprising Sammy who wasn't used to this much activity first thing.

She got herself out of bed and went, purring cat in tow, to make herself a cup of tea, some toast and fill up Sammy's food and water. Her mum was still in bed so Sally enjoyed a quiet breakfast on her lap in the lounge with the morning news on, not really concentrating; trying not to flick over to the cartoons she still enjoyed but tried not to watch since her Mum called them babyish. When she'd finished eating she went to pack her swimming things and make herself a packed lunch, then went and sat back in the lounge to wait.

Her Mum eventually came down at eighteen minutes past eight, still wearing her dirty, white dressing gown and her hair still wet.

"What time we will be going?" Sally asked her, standing up and following her into the kitchen as her mum went to put the kettle on.

"Where?" Her mum asked.

"To activity."

"Again? You only went the other day."

"Activity is on every week," Sally told her, trying not to let her temper rise.

Her mum groaned and put her hand to her head.

"Can't you go get a bus?" Sally's mum said eventually.

"No. I am not allowed to get buses," Sally told her. "You need to do signing in."

"Fine," her mum said, pouring herself a drink, picking up the paper and taking both into the lounge where she sat in the arm chair.

"Okay. What time we will go?"

"What time do we need to go?" Her mum asked in a sarcastic voice.

"We need to be there by eight forty five am. So we need to go at eight thirty am."

"And what's the time now?"

"Twenty five past eight am."

"Oh for God's sake! Fine, we'll go when I've finished my tea!"

They left twenty minutes later and as Sally watched the digital clock's display mark every extra minute they were going to be late, her good mood faltered. But only until they pulled through the iron gates and there, coming out of the doors of the centre along with the rest of the group, was Jimmy. As soon as he saw her he started waving and she waved back as hard as she could; him so relieved she'd made it, her just for seeing him.

The swimming pool they went to was a big one, about fifteen miles or so away from the centre. It wasn't like the swimming pools Sally or Jimmy were used to, ones that were just for swimming. Instead this one was designed to be fun with long, twisting slides of varying speeds, bubbling Jacuzzis and plastic frogs and fishes that sprayed water a good ten meters across the main pool out of spouts hidden in their mouths.

The girls went to get changed in one area, while the boys were together in another. Sally got ready with her back to the other young people, not wanting them to see the slight belly she had and had been secretly trying to loose by doing thirty star jumps every night before she went to bed. She was jealous of most of the care workers; not the older ones like Jean with her graying hair and wide girth, but the younger ones like Mel with their thin waistline, belly button rings and smooth skin. Even their swimming costumes were so much nicer then hers, less revealing then many of the other swimmers, but still enough to be sexy. Sally looked at her own pink t-shirt as she packed it away and tried to subtly rub away the tomato sauce stain on the front as she did.

Once everyone's bags were safely stowed and the care workers had strapped the locker keys around their wrists, they traipsed together over the bumpy, slippery floor, through the little pool of water that was supposed to clean your feet and into the showers where they quickly washed under tepid water.

The boys were already in the first part of the pool, the shallow part where the younger children splashed about between plastic turtles and humped slides that were about two meters long, waiting to be told they could explore.

"We'll meet back here at twelve thirty," Mel called over the echoing din of voices and laughter after everyone had gathered to face her. "Stick in groups of two to one worker please, apart from the one to one's and don't go wandering. Always make sure an adult knows where you are. And enjoy yourselves guys, this is a great place!"

Sally could see Jimmy tense up slightly and she felt herself do the same, looking around to see how many people were watching their little group be given this pep talk.

"Right then, off you go!" Mel said and no one needed to be told twice. Jimmy and Sally stuck together and waded towards the deep end, shadowed by two care workers who watched them go, whilst chatting away about what they'd done last weekend.

"Do you like swimming?" Sally asked Jimmy as the water got to their waists.

"Yes. Can you do handstands?" Jimmy asked. "Like this?" He dove under water and Sally watched as he laid his hands upon the bottom of the pool and forced his skinny legs out the water, holding them straight for a few seconds before tucking them in and re-surfacing.

"That was good," Sally said smiling because he was. "I cannot do them."

"Shall I show you how?"

"Okay."

"You swim under the water and put your hands on the bottom and then put your legs out of the water. Like this," Jimmy said, diving down to demonstrate.

"Now you try," he said once he'd come back up.

Sally dove under water and in two strokes felt the pools tiled floor on her palms. She placed her hands flat and tried to push her legs up, but her hands slipped so she ended up somersaulting instead. She re-surfaced laughing.

"It is hard. Isn't it? It is hard!"

"Yes," Jimmy said.

"Shall we go to the sides and have a rest and then you can show me later?"

"Okay."

They made there way to the side of the pool and found a gap in between other people where they could lean their backs. James and Greg, two other more able lads from the group, were wrestling in the deep bit, trying to trip each other up and dunk each other under the water. Sally laughed as James dived underneath and got hold of Greg's legs before lifting him up, making him fall backwards into the pool, bumping into a teenager with a Celtic band tattooed on his right arm. The teenager turned round and scowled at them, before turning back to the pretty girl that he was talking to.

There were many groups of teenagers in here, Sally noticed, the girls wearing bikinis that were so small they barely covered themselves, parading in front of all the boys with their six pack stomachs, lip rings and baggy swim shorts. Both Sally and Jimmy were enjoying this, being part of a crowd of teenagers, cool looking ones at that.

"Would you like a piercing?" Sally asked, turning to Jimmy.

"Jimmy?" She asked again after getting no reply.

She looked over to him and saw that his attention had been distracted by something behind her. She turned and saw three girls had sat themselves on a thin ledge that ran the length of the pool so that people could rest or smaller children could jump into the water. Sally felt a pang as she watched him look at their smooth legs, tanned skin and toned bodies. They were sitting legs crossed, talking to each other as if they were the only ones in the whole pool, but giving out sly little looks towards the hordes of lads who were pretending that they hadn't noticed them, chucking each other around in a show of masculinity and strength. The girls were pretty, Sally conceded, she just wished that boys would look at her the way Jimmy was looking now.

It didn't take long for one of the girls to notice him looking and give him a deep scowl, an expression Jimmy didn't really get. She then nudged her friends and they all turned to see him looking. One of the three then pushed herself back into the water and with the other two in tow, they all moved towards them. Sally saw Jimmy's cheeks turn red and his eyes flicker, but not leave them as they pushed through the water and the people towards them.

"What are you looking at, perv!" The leader exclaimed when close enough, a brunette girl with high cheek bones and many rings through her ears.

Sally looked at Jimmy whose eyes had gone wide and he'd wrapped his arms round his chest. She thought he was shaking a bit too.

"What, you retarded?" She asked almost spitting out the words.

"He was just looking. Like everyone's looking," Sally said quietly.

"Oh what, this your girlfriend? No one was talking to you," the leader said.

"I am not his girlfriend. I am his friend and we are out on activity," Sally said, trying to keep her gaze sure and steady, unable to meet their eyes though.

"What's going on?" Dave, the support worker who'd stuck near, asked from behind them, having clocked on to the situation, a few moments too late.

"This guy was perving on us," one of the girl's followers said.

"I'm sure he was just looking. Every one looks, just 'cos he doesn't understand he's supposed to do it subtly because of his autism, doesn't mean you can talk to him like that," Dave said.

Sally watched as Jimmy looked away, resting his eyes on the slides to their left, knowing what he was feeling. A mixture of relief and embarrassment that Dave had to talk for them.

"Oh. So he is disabled?" The leader asked.

"Yes, we're a group for disabled children," Dave said, unable to stop himself let a note of pride slip into his tone as he told this to the pretty girls.

"Sorry, we didn't know," the girl said.

"That's okay," Dave said.

"No it is not!" Sally said. "Everyone is looking. Looking is normal."

"Don't worry about it Sally," Dave said, giving the girls a smile. "Come on guys lets hit the slides."

Neither Jimmy nor Sally were sure what he meant by hit the slides, but both were happy enough to walk away from the condescending eyes all around.

The three of them climbed the steps out of the pool and went round to join the queue of people waiting at the stairs to the medium-fast slide's entrance.

"Don't worry mate," Dave said kindly to Jimmy, patting him softly on the back. "Some people don't understand. My Brothers got Autism too and he gets that all the time."

"Okay," Jimmy said in a voice that came out almost like a whisper. "What did they mean by retarded?"

"Yes. I have heard that word before but what does it mean?" Sally asked.

"Don't worry about it. Forget about them and let's have a go on this slide. It's the best one here!"

The queue moved quickly and Sally soon took the advice and forgot about the girls, enjoying instead looking down at all the people who got further and further away as they moved up the steps, shivering from the cold now they were out of the pool. At the top Dave got in position first.

"Listen to the man," he said nodding towards the life guard in a bright red and yellow t-shirt, "and I'll meet you at the bottom." And with that he launched himself into the tube and went shooting towards the bottom. About thirty seconds later and Sally saw him splash into the pool at the other end.

"You go first," Sally said to Jimmy, guiding him into the slide with a gentle hand on his back. She watched as he disappeared from her view, turning into a shadow within the red plastic case of the slide and moving rapidly in the water, before emerging at the other end.

Then it was her turn.

Straight away she felt lifted as she twisted and turned inside. The noise became distant echoes as she built up speed, wishing that she wouldn't have to emerge the other side; that this ride would go on for hours. She smiled as the rest of the pool was blocked out and it was just her and her thoughts whizzing through, water splashing up around her, coming off her feet and into her face.

She came out feeling relaxed and happy with a big splash into the water at the end. She stood up and a little laugh escaped her and she turned smiling to where both Dave and Jimmy were watching.

"Let's go again!" Sally said, stepping out the splash area to where they were waiting.

After they'd got out and changed, the group went up to the café which overlooked the pool. Mel and a couple of the other support workers queued up to get hot drinks for the staff and cold ones for the young adults, even though both Sally and Jimmy would have preferred tea.

Jimmy and Sally were sitting opposite each other at a four person table, with two female support workers who were talking about the traveling that they'd each done to Thailand and New Zealand, whilst Sally and Jimmy stared down at their packed lunches.

"Are you okay?" Sally asked Jimmy who'd been quiet most of the afternoon.

"Yes," Jimmy said, opening up a chocolate bar.

"Have you eaten your sandwiches?" A worker who'd just polished off a plate of chips asked automatically.

"Do you ask that to everyone or is it because I have autism?" Jimmy asked.

"Um… just, normal question mate," the teenaged support worker said.

"Oh. Yes," said Jimmy.

"Okay," said the support worker, turning back to her friend.

"Why did you ask?" Sally asked him.

"I do not understand Sally," Jimmy said shaking his head. "Why did the girls get angry with me when everyone was looking at everyone? Why does having autism mean people get angry and then speak to you like I am stupid?"

"I do not know," Sally said, looking down.

"I do not understand why I am so different. I know it is a New-ro-log-gi-call Con-dit-i-on but why do other teenagers not get shouted at? Why did the girls look at all the boys but not at me?"

Sally looked at her Jimmy and felt stabs in her gut and a tingling in her throat. He tried so hard at everything and seemed to get nowhere.

"Jimmy, can I give you a secret?" She said in a hushed voice, when she was certain the support workers weren't listening.

"Yes."

"I…I also am told I have autism. I do not know why it is hard. I am told it is why I run away sometimes even though I thought I run away to get away from something that is making me un-happy. And why I have to do things in a certain way every time. And why I remember road signs. But my mum also does things in a certain way. She does the same thing every morning. But when I do the same thing it is because I have autism. I do not know why it is different."

"Oh," said Jimmy, lifting his head for the first time since he sat down. "Maybe we could find out together?"

"We could try. All I know is that autism makes things hard and makes people angry or makes them hold your hand and think you cannot do things."

"We can find out together," Jimmy said again, smiling a little now. "It will be nice to have someone to look with."

"Yes," said Sally nodding. "Yes it would."

7

Jimmy woke up on the morning of the 25th of August, just like he always did, at 7:15am to the sounds of his alarm. What was different that morning, however, were the butterflies in his stomach. It was his fifteenth birthday that day and not only did he have the birthday breakfast (Eggs, bacon, tomatoes, beans, waffle and toast) and presents to open, but that evening he was going out to eat with Aalap, Robert and best of all Sally.

His parents hadn't mentioned anything about the night of the party even though Tim knew that they would have been listening out all night. Most likely they'd realized Jimmy had stayed up but not that he got drunk, but anyway, all was good in the house and no one was in trouble. And as such they were all going to Jimmy's favorite Italian restaurant, something they had been liable to miss if they *had* gotten in trouble.

Jimmy waited in bed for a few minutes longer then usual, until it was too un-comfortable to not get up and do things as he normally would. He went downstairs at twenty three past seven and went to make himself a cup of tea, placing everything back in the kitchen, just how he left it. Once the tea was done, he put in two slices of white bread to toast and turned the timer to two and half minutes.

Cup of tea and toast in hand, he went through to their living room. He put the mug down on the glass coffee table and rested the plate on the leather arm rest, then pressed play on the DVD player so he could watch fifteen minutes of Robocop One until quarter to eight. This was a routine he'd picked up from school, since he'd first started when the bus picked him up at twenty past eight and he had time afterwards to brush his teeth along with the other essentials. Since the route had changed however, and the bus picked him up at half past, he'd been a bit lost for the last ten minutes. At the weekend or holidays it was fine, the day started after he'd watched some of the film, but at school once he was ready to go, the ten minutes became him sitting on the sofa waiting for the bus.

His Mum and Dad appeared downstairs at ten to with wide smiles, tinged with just slight irritation.

"Happy birthday!" They called.

"Thank you," said Jimmy smiling.

"We brought your presents into your bedroom, we were hoping you might have stayed as we asked…" His mum said, interrupted by a nudge from his dad. "Sam and Tim are there, do you want to go up? We can do presents then I'll do birthday breakfast, if you're still hungry after toast…"

"Okay," said Jimmy. "I will still be hungry. Birthday breakfast is the best!"

"Good," his mum said, smiling a little more easily now.

"Come on then sport," his dad said as he got up, "let's get you some presents!"

****

Over in her house, Sally was sitting at her computer, staring frustrated at the screen with a small tear in her left eye. She stood up and kicked the old printer which was underneath the desk and had to stop herself from letting the tears flow.

On the screen was the invitation Jimmy had sent her via facebook for the party. She had already told him she was coming, but one thing she had learnt from sitcoms and films… when you go to the party, you take the invite. But hers wouldn't print! She had a while to go before the dinner party, eight and half hours before she had to go and get the bus, but what if it wouldn't work before then?

At eleven am, twenty minutes later, she called Jimmy's house phone number that was at the bottom of the invite in case you wanted to RSVP that way.

"Hello?" A voice called through the receiver.

"Hello Mrs Tiffin, I cannot print off my invitation as my printer is not working."

"Okay. Is this Sally?"

"Yes, this is Sally."

"That's no problem Sally, don't worry about it. You don't need an invitation to come to dinner with us."

"Oh. Okay."

"Do you know where you're going?"

"I am going to go and have some lunch and then watch some television now."

"No, do you know how to get to the restaurant for the meal this evening?"

"Yes. It is opposite the Sainsbury's local shop in town."

"Exactly. We'll see you there at seven?"

"Yes. I will see you then."

Sally put the phone down with a sigh of relief. She wouldn't have to struggle with printing it off after all.

****

Over at the Tiffin household, Jimmy was sitting in the lounge, surrounded by many of the presents that he had been given. Scattered around him were five DVDs, a couple of action figures, three CDs from aunts he had met only once or twice, a book about 'Showdown Pictures' one of his favorite film companies and a couple of posters of his favorite film and TV stars, still wrapped up in plastic.

It was all pretty good, his Mum had chosen two DVDs from his list and even though she had chosen the titles targeted at a younger audience (Madagascar and Wallie) it was altogether a good haul.

He had chosen for the moment to put on 'Dude Where's My Car?' a present from his brother that had warranted a disapproving look from their parents, but one Tim thought was certain to tickle Jimmy. He had tried to watch 'Jaws' that his grandfather had given him (or asked his mum to get for him, since they couldn't make it down this year), but there were too many mistakes in that one for him to be able to get into it properly. The mistakes kept nudging him out of his suspension of disbelief. Jimmy, like some other people with Autism, watched films scene by scene, not taking the film as a whole, but rather as a series of short events. And when too many of these had movie mistakes in them, he got bored waiting for the next one to come around.

Around half an hour into 'Dude Where's My Car?' his mum came in with a mug of hot chocolate with white and pink marshmallows floating and melting on top.

"How's the film?" She asked.

"It is good. It is about a man who says 'where's my car dude?' and the other man says, 'dude, where's your car?'"

"Oh. Sounds… interesting. You happy with all your presents this year?"

"Yes. Thank you for the presents."

"You understand, that although Tim got that new bike and Sam that new consol, we thought you might prefer one or two films."

"Yes. I got four films. They are very good but Jaws had lots of bits wrong so I didn't like it."

"Okay," Mrs Tiffin said, sighing a little. "You don't think it's a little strange you got less then Sam or Tim or than you usually get?"

"I did not get less. Last year I go seven presents and fifteen cards and fifteen pounds and this year I got eight presents and thirteen cards and twenty pounds. You helped me count."

"Okay," Jimmy's mum said, standing up and ruffling his hair. "I think it's strange though."

"Okay," said Jimmy, turning back to the film.

By six O' clock, Jimmy could barely sit still. He was anxious and couldn't sit through 'Wallie,' regressing into childhood habits, he sat next to the DVD player and rewound certain scenes, three, four or five times, drinking in the detail, enjoying the repetition. This used to drive his parents mad and had resulted in them buying him a TV for his room. This had upset his younger, and less understanding brother who didn't understand why an exception to a seemingly age old rule of 'no TVs in the bedroom' had been broken for Jimmy.

But he had thought he'd grown out of this habit some years ago, controlling the urge in the pursuit of becoming an 'adult' and it only became un-suppressible in time of high anxiety or excitement. This would be the first time he would see Sally outside of the clubs. The clubs had finished already; Sally and Jimmy had spent a day together in a farm park that was too young for them and an amusement park that Mel was so stressed about that she didn't want anyone out of her sight. They had got on so well and their parents had even shared the lift run, Sally would take the bus to Jimmy's house and his mum would drive them both to the clubs. But now both were looking towards the prospect of a long school term apart.

Jimmy knew that today he should tell her that he did want to tell people she was his girlfriend, knew that otherwise he wouldn't get a chance to tell her for a long time to come. He just wasn't sure if she felt the same. But it was always the romantics that got the girls in the films so... he had to give it a go.

Aalap arrived first at Jimmy's house first. Since him and Robert couldn't use the buses safely, they were meeting there rather than at the restaurant like Sally was.

"Birthday!" Aalap said to Jimmy as he opened up the door to him, thrusting towards him a card and a neatly wrapped present.

"Thank you," Jimmy said, taking them and going back through to the lounge, with Aalap hot on his heels. In the lounge he sat down on the sofa, his mum pulled out the camera and he opened up the card and the present, smiling when he saw the front cover of 'Starskey and Hutch.'

"Thank you," he said again.

"Okay," said Aalap. "Did you have a good day?"

"Yes."

"Apart from less presents than normal, eh Jim?" His mum said from behind the flash. "It was almost as if one was missing!"

"No, I got more presents then last year. You helped me count," said Jimmy, studying the pictures on the back of the DVD.

One of the bullet points his mum had written on the consent forms for the holiday groups, under 'anything else you'd like to tell us,' was: 'Never take him into a electronic shop. 'He'll spend all day just looking at the backs of DVDs. You won't get him out.' And it was true, even the backs of DVDs had a special allure to Jimmy and he could study each one for tens of minutes.

Robert arrived a few minutes later in a full car as always, three of his five siblings also off somewhere, with his constantly haggard looking mum driving.

"Happy Birthday mate!" He exclaimed as Jimmy opened the door, handing him a card which later turned out to have a DVD voucher inside.

"Thank you," said Jimmy, showing him into the lounge where his family and Aalap were waiting. "Shall we go now and meet Sally at the restaurant?"

"I think we're good to go," his Dad said.

"Got to put some bits in the car," his mum said, nudging his dad.

"Yep, already in the boot," his dad said. "Let's get going."

Sally had been waiting outside the restaurant since six fifteen to make sure she was there on time. She'd put on her favorite green skirt and a black top, put her hair back in a scrunchey and was carrying a black purse that was once her mum's.

When she saw the silver people carrier pull into the car park next to the restaurant at six forty five, her heart jumped with relief that she had got the right place and the right time, invitation or no invitation. Jimmy was there sitting in the back with Robert and Aalap, Jimmy's brothers in the very back on the extra seats and his parents in the front.

She started walking towards them and met the large group at the entrance to the car park.

"Hello Jimmy," she said putting out her hand which he took and shook.

"Hello Sally," he said, not wanting to let go.

"Hello Sally," Robert said coming up to join them, "my name is Robert."

"And I am Aalap," said Aalap.

"Hi again Sally," Mrs Tiffin said. "This is Mr Tiffin, and my other two sons, Sam and Tim."

"Hi," the boys said in unison.

"Right then guys, do you want to go with Mr Tiffin to get our table and I'll be in, in just a minute?"

"Okay," said Jimmy, "let's go."

They all went inside together and waited by the entrance.

"Tiffins!" A large set man called in a smooth Italian accent. "How great to see you. And you've brought friends. I have a table for you, the best table. Is it a birthday, do I remember? Is it the middle one's fifteenth?"

"It is Jimmy's birthday!" Robert said smiling,

"Oh fantastic. I will cook you something extra special," he said, kissing his fingers theatrically.

He took them over to a large table by the window which faced out onto the small front patio with potted plants and smoking tables, and everyone took a seat.

Jimmy loved this restaurant, small enough to be cozy, big enough to feel busy. They had the Italian flag up on the wall along with old farming equipment and pictures of beaches and towns. The waiters and waitresses smiled and the food was just how he liked it.

They sat down and ordered drinks, Tim and his Dad having Italian lager, the others soft drinks. His mum joined them a few minutes later with a large bag she put by her feet. Once they got their drinks, she stood up dramatically and they all hushed.

"Jimmy," she said, "I know you were wondering why you had less presents this year. And I know you thought that was all you were getting. But your father and I thought we'd get you something a bit special this year, something we wanted you to be able to open with all your friends."

She reached down into the bag at her feet and pulled out a present wrapped up in blue, shiny wrapping paper.

"Jimmy, this is for you. Happy birthday."

Jimmy took the gift and put it on the table, slightly disorientated by this strange turn of events, but happy nonetheless.

"Thank you. May I open it?" He asked.

"Go for it!" His dad said.

Jimmy broke into the wrapping paper carefully, under expectant eyes, opening it one flap at a time, peeling back the cello tape, until he could see what was inside. And when he did, his jaw dropped and he looked up at his parents.

"It's a video camera," his mum said, behind her own camera once more, "so that you can start filming things, like we know you want to."

"Wow!" Said Sally, enjoying being part of this moment.

"That is amazing!" Jimmy said. "Now I can start to work in films."

"You can practice with it," said Tim, "and then you can work in films!"

"Thank you!" Jimmy said again, looking at the present, feeling its power in his hands. "Thank you!"

The rest of the evening went smoothly. Jimmy had his Margherita pizza which was as good as always and afterwards the cake his mum had brought in which the waiter put sparklers and candles in. Everyone got on well and Jimmy loved every minute, keeping the camera close by. His mum took loads of snaps including one of him and Sally that she promised to also send to her. When they were all finishing up their drinks and cake he took the camera out of the box and started trying to film, needing Tim to set it up so he could. Then, he filmed the table of his family and friends who waved at him and said a few words. It was such a grown up present, he thought, but best of all, it was the start of his filming career. And he loved being behind the camera as much as he knew he would.

At the end of a perfect evening, they took Sally home first and Jimmy insisted on walking her to the door. He hadn't forgotten what he had wanted to ask, had been thinking about it all the way through dessert. He wanted to tell her that he got Goosebumps when he thought of her and that his heart raced while he was with her. He wanted to tell her how much he was going to miss seeing her at groups every week and how much meeting her had meant to him.

"Sally," he said as she opened the door with her key.

"Yes?"

"I have not told anyone that you are my girlfriend. But…"

"Yes?"

"But… I would not be happy if you told people you had another boyfriend."

"Oh," Sally said blushing, "I have not had another boyfriend since I met you. Or I did not do kissing since I met you," she said looking away now. "Have you?"

Now it was Jimmy's turn to go red. He was happy that she had not kissed anyone else, but he thought back to the party and for the first time, wished his kiss hadn't happened. She was looking at him, smiling, hoping. He hoped she would not want him to have kissed anyone else.

"No," he said.

"That is good," she said.

"Okay, bye Sally."

"Bye Jimmy. I will message you on facebook and see you soon I hope."

"I hope that too," Jimmy said. "I will write to you soon!"

He had a lot of reasons to smile that night, his camera, his meal, his birthday. And Sally. Mostly Sally. For the first time in a long time, he stayed awake until two in the morning, unable to relax, unable to drift off, only able to think about her and how much he was going to miss seeing her on groups.

He felt like he had a partner now. And that meant more to him then anything had done before.

8

Sally was sat on a hard, plastic chair in a sterile corridor of her school. Her legs were pressed tightly together, her hands folded between them and her feet twisted around the legs of the chair but her she held her head resolutely up. Her foot was tapping several times to the second, the noise from this echoed around the long empty corridor. Behind the door next to which she sat she could hear loud voices, dulled a little by the heavy wood it had been made from.

"She's not coming back into my bloody class." She heard.

"Look Jerry, take a seat and tell me what happened."

"Oh! Oh I'll tell you what happened…."

It hadn't been her fault. She hadn't been having a good day, some of the older kids had been teasing her at lunch time, pointing out her dirty clothes and tangled hair. It wasn't her fault she couldn't use the washing machine, the last time she tried she put too much soap in and bubbles had come seeping through the top like in a bugs bunny cartoon.

That day three of the girls in the year above her had come over to where she was sitting on one of the benches that lined the playground and had started calling her tramp girl. It took ten minutes before one of the many milling teaching assistants came over and put a stop to it, telling the girls to leave Sally alone and then mentioning to Sally that she could make more of an effort with her appearance.

So by the time she'd got into art class, she was already wound up. She never really liked art anyway and self portraits were the worst of all. Mr Addler had told the class they had to write three things they liked about themselves within the draw-ing and she couldn't think of anything. So, rather then make stuff up, she just sat at her desk playing with a two pence piece she had found on the floor of the girls' toilets; making it spin and trying to keep that spin going. Mr Addler had tried to rise above it, posing as he did in those corduroy trousers and jacket with that pink scarf wrapped around his neck. But although he liked to think himself cool, he lost his cool pretty quickly.

"Sally, will you put down that coin and do some work!" He shouted at her eventually.

"Don't want to," Sally had said towards the desk behind which she sat.

"Excuse me young lady! You will do as you're told. Now draw a picture."

"No," Sally had said. "I don't understand. I want to draw something else."

"It's not up to you what you draw," Mr Addler had said as Sally span the coin again, using her thumb and forefinger. "Now draw!"

He had then picked up her pencil and jabbed it towards her hand and, whether he meant to or not, the sharp end had stabbed her in-between her knuckles. At this point she had stood and planted a right hook onto his cheekbone. And that is why she now sat on this chair, listening to the accusing voice tell the head teacher what had happened.

"Calm down Jerry, I'm sure it was an accident."

"Some accident! The little bitch hit me good!"

Sally felt every muscle in her body twitch at that word. She hated that word, more than any other word.

"Jerry, calm down now! I will not have my pupils be called by that word."

"What, bitch? What else am I going to call her. That's what she is Helen, you just remember this isn't the first time..."

Their voices were getting fainter now, becoming murmurs like the sea heard from a hotel on the seafront, or the laughter and chatter you hear from a swimming pool changing room. Sally ran her hand over the sky blue wall, feeling all the lines and bumps of imperfect painting beneath her fingers. She could only see two choices; go in there and hit him again, or get away as fast as her legs would take her.

No one said a word as she moved through reception, her head down counting the tiles as she went. No one said a word as the doors parted to let her through into the cool October afternoon or as she walked into the car park. The whole way she waited for someone to stop her, but when that hand never came and she had reached the gate, she put two hands on the top, lifted herself up so she was sitting on it, swung her legs around and dropped down on the other side to freedom.

Once out the grounds, without looking back, she followed the twisted concrete path with weeds that sprouted through, all the way to the main road, where she crossed over at the traffic lights. On the other side of the road was a park, lined with woods and it was here that she found herself, three minutes and thirty seven seconds after leaving that hard backed chair. She made her way to the back of this little wooded area to a wire fence that was completely covered from view and sat down with her back against it. Then she bent her knees up to her chin, folded her arms over them, put her head upon her arms and let the tears flow free from where they'd been hiding, behind those soft, blue eyes.

****

Sally spent the next two days off school. At the end of the second day she sat on her bed waiting patiently in her room, cat on her lap, reading a dog eared cook book, looking over the recipes that she knew by heart. She had a Sony walkman by her side, headphones in her ears and was listening to radio one.

This routine was familiar, but she didn't feel comfortable. She didn't like that downstairs there were five people, two of whom she'd not met until today and that *they* were deciding *her* next steps *for* her. She'd been asked her opinion, the new social worker had come to see her quickly and had thrown a lot of words towards her that she hadn't understood, words like funding, respite and residential and what would she think of these? Sally hadn't wanted to appear stupid in front of the young lady so she'd agreed when she knew she was supposed to and shaken her head when that was what was expected. Now all she could do was wait for them to call her down and tell her what would be happening to her.

She closed the recipe book and got out some plain paper, using the closed book to lean on. And then she wrote out from memory the recipe for a roasted vegetable lasagna, first drawing out a template so it looked the same as the one in the book and then writing in the words.

About half an hour later she heard feet on the stairs, disturbing and adding a strange beat to her music. Then a short sharp knock at her door. She didn't answer straight away, collecting her breath, she started counting towards ten, but got only to seven before the door was opened.

"Can you come join us please Sal?" The social worker asked, speaking slowly and deliberately.

"Okay," Sally said, putting her walkman back in her bedside cabinet, with the book and three written out recipes.

Downstairs in the kitchen the five people were sitting around the kitchen table drinking tea from chipped mugs. She knew her mum, of course, the head teacher at her old school and the lady from Connexions who sometimes came to her school and asked her what she wanted to do when school was finished. She'd met the social worker earlier, but the other person she hadn't been introduced to.

"Okay then," the Social worker said as Sally took a seat between her mum and the lady from Connexions, "I'd like to introduce you to everyone who you don't know."

"I know everyone," Sally said quietly.

"Have we met before?" The lady opposite her asked.

"Yes," Sally said, not wanting to seem stupid.

"I'm not sure we have. I'm the head teacher over at Hollygrove's school. My name is Mrs Dorite."

"I know," said Sally.

"What we'd like to say, is how would you feel about coming to our school?"

"For a visit? I could see Jimmy, that would be nice."

"No, she means going to her school permanently. To learn, like you did at our school," Helen, the head teacher from Glen Park said.

"Why?" Sally said. "My friends go there and that is my school. Why would I go to another school?"

"Because... because of the trouble we've been having recently," Helen said.

"We think you'll be more comfortable in Hollygroves," the Social worker interjected. "It's for people who need a bit more support, like we think you do. You've run away from school five times now."

"They mean they've got higher fences," Sally's Mum said laughing. She wasn't happy that her afternoon had been taken away from her like this. "You guys have security guards as well? Then maybe you can control her."

"It's not about that," Mrs Dorite said quickly towards Sally. "It's just that you will be happier there."

"Do I choose?" Sally asked.

"I'm afraid not," Helen said. "The paperwork's already gone through. We can't support you anymore at our school, what with the running away and the violence. I'm afraid it's Hollygrove's or an out of borough, residential placement."

"Can I look?"

"Sorry," the social worker said, "they're just too expensive. It's Hollygroves or nothing Sally."

"Okay," Sally said.

"You start on Monday."

"Okay," Sally said, still not really understanding.

They all stayed a while longer, sometimes they asked Sally questions but Sally wasn't in an answering mood. She should have been used to the barrage of questions by now; she had social worker visits every month or so, and every four or five months she'd get a new social worker and had to say the same things again, answer the same questions, tell all the stories. She was usually comfortable enough talking to these professionals, but at the moment all she could concentrate on was that her school was no longer he school. It wasn't as if she was happy there, she knew she'd been in trouble a few times and even had to spend a few days away from school before, but never leave completely. To Sally the people around the table seemed to be talking a million words a minute and all she wanted to do was ask questions like;

"What about my work?"

"Would I have a window seat at school?"

"What about the hopscotch grid on the playground, is there one at the new school?"

"Do I still get to see my friends?"

"What about that picture of me up on the wall doing cooking, can that go up in the new school?"

But there was too much that needed to be said and too many forms to fill out to get around to questions like those.

9

Jimmy was sitting in his 'outing' class, talking about the films he was making with his birthday present, with Robert and Aalap when he saw her come in. It made no sense to see her in a place so out of place. She was someone who he saw outside school, in club doing activities or for his birthday, so much so that it took him a while to really understand it was her. There were these three places for Jimmy; school, home and outside of home. Occasionally there were holidays abroad and these were always strange to him and he didn't count them because when he thought about them and tried to think of all the places to go on holiday, his head hurt. This was a feeling not dissimilar. It was a bit like when he saw teachers when he went into town or went to a restaurant with his family and he kept his eyes down and ignored them, even if it was one of the ones he got on well with in school. They always spoke to him and were always a bit put out when he didn't really respond, but they were just out of place.

But he couldn't ignore Sally. It was Sally. He was feeling all these things at once and it made him feel strange, so he focused back on his work and kept his head down.

"Oh, hiya Sally," the class teacher, Mrs Jacobs, said to her.

"Hi."

"Everyone, stop what you're doing for a minute. This is our new student Sally. She's just moved over to us from Glen Park School. I want everyone to make her feel very welcome. Where would you like to sit Sally?"

But Sally didn't answer. She glanced up to Jimmy and they made eye contact, briefly, before both looked away.

"She can sit by me!" A voice called out from across the room. Jimmy looked over to see Charlie waving at her. "Unless she wants to sit next to her boyfriend, Jimmy?"

Sally looked over at him and blushed, then looked back to Jimmy who was blushing too and not looking at her. A few of the guys in the class were sniggering, looking between the two of them.

"Sally's not my girlfriend..." Jimmy started, wanting to explain about their pact to not have other partners, but before he could Sally said:

"No, Jimmy's not my boyfriend," looking at the floor.

"Okay," Mrs Jacobs said, taking back the reigns on the situation, "there's a spare seat by Charlie, have you met him before?"

"Yes, I do art club with him."

"Okay, over you go then."

Sally went and took a seat next to the smug looking Charlie, who conspicuously pattered her on the back as she did. She glanced over to Jimmy who was looking at them, looking upset,

Sally thought. But then he had said she wasn't his girlfriend. Maybe she hadn't understood the other night, she thought. She'd been wrong about her school being her school, so maybe Jimmy wasn't her man, maybe he just wanted to be friends. Suddenly she was glad she was sitting next to Charlie. For all his faults at least she knew he found her attractive.

At lunch time they all filled out the room together. Jimmy hung back so he could talk to Sally, wanting to clear the air.

"Hi Sally," he said, "are you here to visit?"

"Hi Jimmy," she replied, "no, I'm coming to school here now. My other school said they could not handle me so I need to go here where they have more higher fences."

"Oh," said Jimmy as it dawned on him the hugeness of this. She was coming to his school now. He would see her every day, in the playground, in the lessons, on trips and even at the discos the school held once a term. He started beaming, his upset wearing off quickly. "That is good."

"Yes, it is very excellent," Charlie said, opening the door for Sally as they moved towards the hall.

"Where are we going now?" Sally asked the lads.

"To the hall for lunch darling," Charlie said, "it is silver class's turn now darling so we are going to go do eating."

"Oh," Sally said, "okay."

The hall felt crowded although the lunches were staggered and only a third of all the school was there. Jimmy, Sally, Charlie, Aalap and Robert all sat together round one table near the fold-away climbing frame.

"What have you got for lunch today then Sally?" Charlie asked.

"I have cheese and tomato sandwiches and crisps," Sally said, pulling the packets out of her bag.

"I have cheese and pickle sandwiches and some chocolate and some olives and some dunkers," Charlie said, lining them up on the table.

"Sally…" Jimmy started. They all looked up at him, but he couldn't think of anything to say. He found himself hating Charlie a bit for how easy he found it to talk to people, especially girls. He was always the one who had a girlfriend at school. Even now his ex-girlfriend Emma who he'd been with all summer but had broken up with two weeks ago, was staring at them, looking angry. She was in an older year at school and someone a lot of the boys fancied. Jimmy didn't know how he did it.

"Sally, are you happy you are here?" Charlie said.

"Yes. It is okay."

"Well, after we have done eating I will show you around the playground."

"Okay. Will you come as well Jimmy?"

They all looked at Jimmy who nodded.

"Okay then, you can come to," Charlie said, nodding. "You can come outside with us."

So, after they had finished, they put away their things and got ready for their break as Gold class made their way into the hall. Robert and Aalap were on register duty, they had to go get the registers for the afternoon period, so they headed off down the corridor whilst Jimmy, Sally and Charlie headed outside.

Out in the playground, the first thing Jimmy noticed was the height of the fences. He'd not paid them much attention before, was used to them after six years here. He wondered why Sally needed such high fences and thought it was probably because her mum was scared of the bad people who sometimes hung around playgrounds and tried to take children that weren't theirs. Jimmy had never seen any of these people himself, but he had been told about them many times.

"Is this different to your old school?" Charlie asked Sally with a wink.

How did he do that? Jimmy wondered.

"Yes. The people are louder and are more special need. We had no wheelchairs in our old school. And everyone could talk."

"Oh," said Charlie, putting an absent hand around her waist as they walked over to some picnic benches next to one of the fences. Jimmy saw and felt tight pangs in his stomach and an urge to take his hand away from her waist. Sally glanced over at him, she was feeling un-comfortable, but this was a new school and she wanted to fit in and Jimmy said he didn't want her to be his girlfriend so she was sure he wouldn't mind.

"Are you coming to art club next week Sally?" Charlie asked.

"Yes."

"I am going to be a great artist when I am older. What are you going to be?"

"I don't know," Sally said, "Jimmy's going to be a film man though. He knows everything about films." She turned to him, smiling. "Tell us something about films?"

"Okay," said Jimmy, "do you know…" But his mind had gone blank. What should he say? The Matrix was released in 1999? That during love actually the word actually is said twenty two times? That there have been seven James bond actors?

"I don't know," Jimmy said, feeling his cheeks turn red. Why didn't he know? Why couldn't he think all of a sudden?

"I like pirates of the Caribbean," Charlie said.

"Me too," Sally said. "I like Jack Sparrow. He fights a lot with his sword."

"Yes. Jack Sparrow is very good," Charlie said. "Here we are darling, the benches. I am going to go toilet, I will be back in a minute."

Once Charlie had left, Jimmy and Sally found themselves looking around the playground awkwardly; watching some people play on their own, some people organize a football game and some just sitting with staff.

"Is Charlie going to be your boyfriend?" Jimmy asked after a while.

"I don't know," Sally said. "He was before. And you said you weren't my boyfriend."

"Oh. But I thought we weren't going to have other boyfriends or girlfriends?"

"That is what I thought. But then you said we weren't going to be boyfriend and girlfriend. And Charlie is okay."

"Yeah, well," Jimmy said, his temper rising, a rare thing, "well, I kissed a girl at Tim's party, so that is okay then."

Sally turned to him and he instantly regretted saying it, seeing the way her face contorted.

"You said you had not done kissing with girls since you met me! You told a lie!"

"But... I am sorry," Jimmy said, "but you told a lie when you said we were not going to have other boyfriends!"

"But then you said..." Sally started, but couldn't finish, she was too stressed. She had hated having to leave her school and the only good thing was that Jimmy was going to be at the new one. Just then Charlie came back onto the playground, so Sally just picked up her bag and jogged to him.

Jimmy watched her go with a hollow feeling in his stomach, he had been so happy when he realized she was coming here. Now it seemed she didn't feel like he did, it had all been fruitless.

By the time Aalap and Robert came over to join him, he was in a bad mood and they couldn't understand why. He stayed like that for the rest of the day, not talking to Sally or Charlie. His friends hoped it wasn't going to be like this for the rest of school.

10

Sally hadn't slept much that night. She had had intermittent periods of dozing, but mostly she'd stared up at the ceiling thinking about Jimmy, absent mindedly stroking the purring Sammy who'd made himself comfortable by Sally's side.

Last evening at the art club Charlie had made a pass at her. He had come up behind her while she was at the computer and put an arm around her. He had told her she was beautiful which made her blush and helped her feel good inside. But then when he tried to kiss her, she stopped him. Even though she wanted it, even though it made her feel pretty, she hadn't let him kiss her. And it was all for Jimmy. All of it. She'd do anything for him, she realized. She might not always understand what people were thinking and had trouble thinking from other people's point of view. But she knew that if she kissed him, and Jimmy found out, he wouldn't talk to her ever again. She knew from the way he had been just from when her and Charlie were talking, that if she had lent in to kiss him, that would have been it for her and Jimmy. And she couldn't handle that. She realized she needed Jimmy to like her so that she could be happy. She needed him and that scared her.

She got up, went downstairs, fed the cat and made herself a cup of tea. She felt more awake then she normally would at this time in the morning, more focused on the day ahead. She had to patch things up with Jimmy; he was the one she wanted, not Charlie. Charlie wasn't a nice guy, when they'd been together she knew he'd kissed at least two other girls. She knew she shouldn't stay hanging around him just because he made her feel pretty. But she was so confused by her and Jimmy's relationship... were they together, were they just friends or were they friends who didn't have other girlfriends or boyfriends? She couldn't work it out.

At 8:30 the bus came and she got on, taking a seat by herself at the window so she could stare out and visualize the next road signs and make the journey more comfortable. She knew most of them already and got angry with herself when she envisaged a 'stop' sign that turned out to be a 'slow' sign.

At school, the teaching assistants met them in the car park and shepherded them into the building and to their various classrooms for morning registration. In her class she saw Jimmy, Robert and Aalap were sitting where they always did, half way back on the left hand side of the room, talking together in low voices. Jimmy looked up as she came in and she smiled at him, he smiled a half smile back, then looked to her seat, next to Charlie, who had also noticed her come in and was beckoning her over. But she didn't go that way, didn't want to be near him after last night, so she went and took a seat in the middle of the room, something that made her feel less comfortable because of the change, but yet more comfortable because she was nearer Jimmy.

They were doing money skills that morning but Sally could barely concentrate on working out the totals of all the different coins on the sheet of paper in front of her. She found money difficult, working out what would cost what and why, placing values on the pictures before her. Normally, because she understood the importance of knowing about money to be an adult, this would be the kind of lesson where she concentrated, but instead she found her eyes straying to Jimmy who was trying to do the task with Robert and Aalap.

Time just didn't seem to be moving; she just wanted it to be ten thirty so she could talk to Jimmy in the playground away from his friends and Charlie.

Things went from bad to worse however when Mrs Gregory called the lesson to an end and asked Sally to go and get the register for the after break registration.

"But I will be late for break time?" Sally said.

"Yes, but we all have to do it. It's the whole class's responsibility…" Mrs Gregory replied.

"But…but…"

"But what Sally?"

"Okay," she said eventually, "I will go get the register."

When she'd packed away her things, she practically ran down the corridor towards the reception where the registers were kept. She had to wait for Henry from the class below her to pick *that* class's register up first and he was struggling to choose the right one, even though they were color coordinated.

"Please can I get the silver one?" Sally asked the assistant who was helping Henry.

"You need to wait your turn," she was told.

"But I need to go and do break time!"

"So do we all," the assistant said in an exaggeratedly exasperated voice.

Finally, register in hand Sally paced back along the bright corridors to her class room and handed it to Mrs Gregory, who was sitting at her desk drinking tea. Then she turned and headed for the playground.

By the time she got out to the playground, her blood pressure was high, she was nervous. She spotted Robert and Aalap sitting on one wooden bench, chatting to each other and Jimmy and Charlie on the bench next to them deep in conversation. She picked up her pace to almost a jog across the playground towards the latter pair and as she got near, both boys looked up at her.

"Hi Jimmy," Sally said, waving.

But Jimmy didn't respond; he just stared at her, tears welling up in his eyes.

"Hi baby," Charlie said giving her a wink. "I was just telling Jimmy about our kiss yesterday and how good it was and how we are now girlfriend and boyfriend baby."

Sally froze. It hadn't happened, why was Charlie lying like this? She looked from him to Jimmy, then back to him.

"But we did not do kissing last night," she said slowly.

"Yes we did," Charlie said, "we did it before and we did it then. We did some kissing in the art club. Shall we do some more kissing now?"

"But..." She started,

"I... I ..." Jimmy said, his cheeks darkening, his muscles clenching, "I..."

"Jimmy, me and Charlie..." Sally started, but suddenly lost the words. She looked at him again and hated how sad he looked. So she did what she did best when she was upset. She started to run.

"Wait," Jimmy said, having seen the tears start to fall off Sally's face. He chased after her as she ran down the playground, along the side of the school. The abundant teaching assistants seemed not to notice as they both sped towards the only part of the playground hidden from easy view, the fence that backed onto the car park.

"Wait!" He shouted again as she reached and started climbing the fence that was higher than at her last school, but not high enough.

"Stop," he called, but she was at the top by the time he had got to the bottom. Jimmy looked up at the fence, then over to Sally as she dropped down the other side and in that instant his fear dissipated and he put his foot into the first of the links of the chain fence and hurled himself up, step by step.

By the time he got to the floor Sally was already out of the car park, charging down the road in the general direction of her old school, wanting to find the place she used to hide. She glanced over her shoulder just once and saw that Jimmy was in close pursuit. She wanted to stop and keep going at the same time. She turned the corner and saw some bushes on the side of the road, which she pushed her way into.

"Sally!" She heard him call, but she just put her hands over her ears; pushing and climbing further into the thicket.

"Sally. Sally where did you go?"

She pushed all the way in until she found a clearing, wide enough for her to sit down, amongst the weeds, brambles and nettles. Then, she let the tears flow more freely, put her bag into her lap and hugged it as tight as she could.

It didn't take long for Jimmy to find her. He had glanced her going into the bushes, saw her pink bag as she had gone. He had made his way in straight away, braving the nettles and thorns that were all around and had grown up to a foot high.

When he found her, her arms were clasped tightly around her knees, her bag was in her lap and her forehead was resting on her arms. Her hair had fallen over her arms and it looked to Jimmy like a golden waterfall.

"Hi Sally," he said and saw that her shoulders were shaking. He went and sat down next to her and put his arm around her to try and stop them from doing that. He felt her shoulders loosen as he did and she leaned into him, just a little bit. They sat like that for about five minutes while Jimmy tried to get the words the right way round in his head.

"Sally, I know you kissed Charlie. But I know that, that's okay because I kissed a girl at my brother's party and it was nice because I had not done it before and it was nice because people kiss you if they like you and I want people to like me. But I didn't like thinking about you kissing him."

Sally looked at him, resting her cheek on her arms now. He wasn't smiling but his face was soft, comforting.

"Jimmy, I did not kiss Charlie. I said no. I am sorry if it upset you."

"You did not kiss him?"

"No."

"I believe you," he said and she could see that he meant it.

"Thank you," she said.

"I am sorry for being upset."

"I am sorry too," Sally said, smiling at Jimmy whose face was now so close to hers.

Then, suddenly, he was leaning forwards towards her and she was leaning into him. When their lips finally met, both felt their stomachs turn in a way neither had felt before. As they kissed, a passionate, if slightly awkward kiss, Jimmy felt every hair on his body tingle and stand on end, he felt nothing and everything at once, it was like a dream to him that he never wanted to stop. Sally never thought anything could feel this good, not just take the upset away, but actually make her feel happy, happier then she could remember, safer, more secure, more uplifted. In his arms like this, she knew she could achieve anything, autism or no.

When they'd stopped they looked into each other eyes for a moment and smiled, then Sally hugged him tightly to her, while he stroked her hair from around her eyes back around her ears.

"Sally I..." Jimmy started.

"Sally! Jimmy! Out here now!" A teacher's voice cut through their moment. Both had forgotten it was a school day.

II

Jimmy was sitting in the front room of his house staring into a television that wasn't quite black. His eyes were wet, but not with sadness. Sally had got the brunt of the shouting at school because she had a history of running away. Jimmy had wanted to stick up for her but couldn't find the words. Both Jimmy's parents and Sally's mum had been called into school and had to have a private chat with Mrs Dorite. When Jimmy's mum came out she gave Jimmy a hug. Sally's mum had grabbed her by the collar and pretty much dragged her outside. Jimmy had been told by his parents he wasn't allowed to see Sally again, apart from at school. He had protested but to no avail.

Now he was listening to his parents talking in the other room.

"It was her, her bad influence. He's such a good boy normally," his mum was saying. "Oh, what are we going to do Paul?"

"He's okay. Just keep a tighter leash on him is all."

"But he doesn't understand, can't understand. He could have been hit by a car or anything…"

It was then that Jimmy had, had enough. Fed up of people talking about him behind closed doors, fed up of people thinking he didn't understand. He knew what he was doing when he'd climbed that fence. It was more important to him to follow her than to stick to the rules. He'd made his own decision. When Tim had run away from home a few years back when his parents had caught him drunk at fourteen, they'd shouted at him for fifteen minutes. Jimmy wished they'd do the same for him, wished they'd let him take responsibility for his actions.

"Not Sally's fault," He shouted at them.

They both turned, surprised, Jimmy's Dad almost dropped his tea; they hadn't heard him come in.

"Jimmy, your father and I need to talk; we need to figure out what we're going to do."

"But you don't know anything," Jimmy shouted.

"Please Jimmy! I've had a bad day, had to leave a meeting because your little friend made you leave school and I'm not in the mood!" Jimmy's dad shouted.

"You could have been killed," Jimmy's mum added, standing from the dining room table.

"I know about roads!" Jimmy shouted.

"You have autism!" His mum said. "That means you have no sense of danger."

"I know danger," Jimmy said, his voice quieting.

"Your room now!" Jimmy's dad shouted. "Now, young man, we need to talk."

"But... but, you don't know!" Jimmy said, his blood heating as the words became more difficult to say. "I have autism... but that does not... I do not know..." He said, his head beginning to spin.

"No of course you don't, and that's the problem," his mum said, shaking her head. "Go to your room Jimmy, *we* will figure this out."

Up in his room, Jimmy was furious. He tossed and he turned on top of his bed, wishing he knew what was going on, wishing he could talk to Sally about all this. Why was everything so different for people like them, who went to schools like they did? Why when he did something wrong was it because of his autism? Why not because he loved Sally and she was sad? Why when someone at school hit someone else was it because they didn't understand, but when it happened in the news it was because they were thugs? Jimmy understood some of the people at school really didn't understand, but a lot of them did and most of them knew it was wrong to hit but did it anyway, just like the people in Tim's school or the people in the news.

One day, he thought to himself, *I will find out. Even if it takes me the rest of my life. I will find out.*

12

Sally was confused again, sitting at her kitchen table with Mrs Dorite, her mum, a social worker, the careers and education adviser, a woman she didn't recognize and inexplicably, but perfectly okay by her, her favorite aunt, Tracy.

"So..." Sally started, prompting six heads to swivel towards her, but when the words didn't come immediately, the eternally busy assembled group moved on, only Tracy was left smiling at her niece.

"Have you seen the school?" The social worker asked her mum, making notes in the huge pile of paperwork stacked before her.

"No," her mum said, pulling out a packet of Mayfair cigarettes from her bag and lighting one.

"Don't you think that's a problem?" The social worker asked.

"Do I ..." Sally tried.

"Of course not. Do we have a choice?" Her mum said.

"I guess not,"The social worker said.

"So Sally, are you looking forward to coming to us?" The lady Sally didn't recognize asked.

"I…" Sally said, but again words didn't come in time.

"We don't have a choice, I'm afraid," the lady from the education service interjected. "Sally's made her way through all the local schools, the residential options are too expensive and are a route we'll go down only if this placement doesn't work. And since…"

"Okay, so Sally is all this okay with you?"Tracy asked deliberately slowly.

"I don't know," Sally said.

"Well, as we've mentioned, there's no choice," Mrs Dorite said. "I'm sorry Sally, you've got a history of this kind of thing and if you're going to be putting our students in danger…"

"No!" Sally shouted, losing patience. "I don't know what is happening.This is my home. I stay with AuntTracy in some holidays. Not while I go to school. And my school is with Jimmy and Robert and Aalap and Charlie and not in Surrey…"

"Well Sally,"Tracy said, slowly and sweetly, "you have to go to *a* school until you are sixteen and you are fifteen.You can't stay in the school with Jimmy because you broke the rules. And there are no other schools you can get to from your house with your mum. So you have to stay with me for a while so you can go to a school near me. Mum will join us later, once she's sorted her things down here."

"And if you like it, you can stay on at our sixth form," Mrs Ferrell, head teacher of Linding School said.

"Does that sound okay?"Tracy asked.

"Okay," said Sally. "Can I still talk too Jimmy?"

"Of course darling, we've got a phone, the internet, you can write and if he's allowed, he can come up and stay."

"God," Sally's mum muttered under her breath, turning away when the others looked at her.

"So we're all okay here?" The social worker asked, still writing notes as quick as she could, glancing towards the relevant people.

"I think so," the lady from careers and education responded.

"Yep," the head teacher said.

"Yes," Mrs Dorite said.

"Good. Then let's get the paperwork filled out and we can move on with all this," she said, handing around forms to fill in for everyone but Sally.

****

At half twelve that night Sally was once again staring at the ceiling, nauseas, anxious, every muscle tensed, her teeth grinding upon one another, over and over again, uncontrollable.

She understood a few things about what had happened that day, which she listed over in her head, trying to make them more ordered, but finding no peace within their forms.

She would be moving schools again.

She would be going to live with her aunt.

Her bedroom would be a new bedroom.

She would not come back, apart from in the holidays and only then until her mum moved up to join them.

She would only see Jimmy in the holidays. If Jimmy's parents let him.

She was going in one day's time and staying for good.

She would not be able to say goodbye to Jimmy.

Over and over she thought these things, for more then an hour, but the more she thought the less sense she could make of it. Why, when she was finally happy in a school, did she have to leave? She only ran away when she was sad, she wouldn't be sad at school anymore, not now she knew how Jimmy felt.

As carefully as she could she swung her feet from under her covers and got herself out of bed.

She couldn't not say goodbye to Jimmy. She had to see him before she left, before she was taken away. Maybe he could help her make more sense of all this. Maybe he could make it so she might stay.

She slipped some jeans on under her nightie then put a blue hooded top on, quietly as she could, knowing that if her mum was to hear her, she'd never let her go. Then she crept out onto the dark landing, placing each foot carefully and purposefully on the worn carpet. All the lights in the house were off, even the one behind her mum's door which was ajar in the frame.

At the top of the staircase she felt about the darkness for the handrail, finding it after a few seconds and using it to guide herself down to the front door, which she opened with a click that seemed louder then usual.

Outside the cold hit her as she stepped off her doorstep and onto her portion of the estate. She turned and started walking quickly along the houses, cutting across the small green with its broken slide, so she could avoid the ally where quite often teenaged boys and girls would hang out, shouting things at passers by.

She got onto the main street, looked both ways, then turned right, recognizing the traffic light sign that marked the start of the journey to Jimmy's, one she had done when she'd got the bus to his a couple of times over the holidays so that Jimmy's mum could take them together to the activity groups, once their parents had decided to share the lifts.

The streets were dark and empty. She walked purposefully, enjoying the structure of the journey for the most part, ticking off the road signs in her head as she passed each one, 'Stop' signs, 'give way' signs, and '40mph' signs as she hit the pavement that ran along the duel carriage way.

A few times the streets weren't empty though. The first time this happened was alongside the duel carriageway and there were three of them, teenage lads staggering along together, talking loudly, holding cans of lager which they swigged from. Sally knew all about stranger danger and drunkenness, but there were streetlights and plenty of cars buzzing by so when they got near she flattened herself against the wall and the teenagers just walked straight past.

The second time, however, was sometime after she had turned off the busy street and into the side road (turning off just after a sign that introduced the road as 'Gainsbury Avenue') where from a distance she could hear more loud voices, at least three different ones, boys and girls and this time without any squeak in their voices, so Sally deduced they were older. It was a quiet, expensive residential street lined with hanging trees on the verges and large, dark, front gardens outside impressive

Tudor style, or larger red brick houses. The streetlights were at long intervals and not a single light in a window was on, making the shadows dark and the areas of real light scarce. The street was a long and winding one, Sally didn't know when the voices would reach her, but she knew they were getting closer. Her heart in her mouth, she decided the only option was to hide. She crept quietly into a front Garden on her left, moving quickly and keeping low next to a black BMW that was parked on a concrete drive in front of a double garage. She tiptoed around to the front of the car, parked about a meter away from the garage, and ducked down low.

The voices got louder and louder and her breathing got quicker and quicker, so loud she got worried they'd hear, she pressed her head against the smooth car, which was nice and cold, damp from the evening's earlier rain and then she closed her eyes.

She didn't open them again until the voices were well off in the distance and were drowned out by the rolling, far off traffic. Then she got out from her hiding place and carried on up the road.

She got to Jimmy's house half an hour later and stood outside. She knew she couldn't just ring the bell, she knew that his mum would not be happy with her getting here at this late time. She just had to figure out a way to get inside or to get his attention without anyone knowing or seeing. But she didn't know which room was his and she could see no way of ascending the house or breaking in through a window.

As she scanned the house, knowing he was within the walls, knowing he was so close but just out of reach, something seemed to break inside her. If she shouted he'd hear, but so would his mum and she wouldn't let them talk, probably just take her straight home again. But at least he would hear. Did she have a choice?

Just as she was ready to let loose, however, she heard yet more voices coming along the suburban street and she quickly dived for cover within Mrs Tiffin's well tended front garden, pushing her way into a thick, spiky bush that separated theirs and their neighbor's gardens.

The voices, again teenaged, were slurred and getting louder. This time there was no car to lean on, so she shut her eyes and pushed her hands to her ears to try and block as much of it as she could. She could still hear the voices though her hands, they were getting louder and louder until they seemed to be right next to her, two or three people talking and laughing.

When Sally was younger she used to hum. It was a habit she had picked up when she got nervous, her fingers in her ears, humming loudly to block out the world. She'd weaned herself off doing it to avoid the strange looks she'd get when she did it, but sometimes, sometimes it still happened without her noticing. And it was happening now. As soon as she noticed, she stopped, moved her hands from her ears and dared to open her eyes to see a strange, spiky haired man peering into the bushes. Instantly she froze, fear coursed through her body as this pierced, punky man stared at her and she stared back, wide eyed, unable to move.

The man blinked, then blinked again. Then he smiled, finally having seen Sally through the gloom.

"Yo!" He said in a muffled voice, "Mate, does your mum keep fairies in your garden?"

"Nah man, they all moved away when I was five. Why?" Came a reply.

"Well I think one's come back. There's a girl in your bushes mate."

"What!" Tim's voice came back, louder then he meant it to and he shushed himself. "Let me see."

Tim's face appeared a few moments later, peering into the bushes. Sally recognized him as Jimmy's brother from his birthday and relaxed just a bit, at least he wasn't a stranger. But on the other hand he might tell Jimmy's mum she was here.

"You okay?" He asked Sally's shadowed figure. "Can you hear me? Do you need an ambulance?"

An ambulance would take her home, Sally knew this. She had to take a chance and trust him...

"Hello Tim," she said stepping out of the bushes.

"Sally! What are you doing here?" Tim asked, under his breath.

"I have to move to my aunt's tomorrow and go to a new school and I won't see Jimmy anymore and I wanted to see him and I will miss him and my mum wouldn't let me visit so I walked here."

"You walked here?"

"I'm confused. This is your brother's girlfriend?" The punky guy asked.

"Mate, I don't know. You know what it's like at their age. Look," he said turning back to Sally, "my mum will not be happy if she finds you or hears us, you will be in loads of trouble. I'll call you a taxi, it'll take you home then you can call us tomorrow and come and visit before you go."

"But my mum will not let me!"

"Well... look, my mum knows everything, she'll catch you then make you go home anyway..."

"But I need to see Jimmy before I go!" Sally said, willing away tears that were starting to show in her eyes.

"Look, I'm in enough trouble at the moment..."

"Ah, come on dude! You can't stand in the way of true love!" The punky friend said, dramatically holding his heart.

"Please Tim," Sally said sincerely, looking at Jimmy's older brother and knowing that he would help but not knowing why she knew that, not noticing the friendliness or softness in his face that was similar to what she saw in Jimmy's.

"But... oh, god, go on then," Tim said holding a hand to his forehead. "I'll let us in, call a taxi, you can have ten minutes with Jimmy and then you gotta go when the car arrives. Man, if we get caught I'm in more trouble then ever. I won't see daylight again. You have to be dead quiet."

"Okay," Sally said, smiling now.

"Worth it mate," the punky man said, putting his hand against the door frame to steady himself. "Well worth it."

Tim got out his keys and after a couple of jabs in the direction of the keyhole, managed to open up the door and let them in. He turned to his friend and pointed in the direction of the kitchen, put his fingers on his lips for them both, then took Sally's hand, leading her up the stairs, treading each one carefully.

Sally moved slow, determined not to wake anyone up and they reached the top of the stairs with the house still dark and quiet. Tim led her to Jimmy's room and they went inside.

Jimmy was asleep in his bed, so Tim gently shook him awake.

"Jimmy," he whispered as he shook him. Jimmy opened his eyes and looked up at his brother. "Jimmy, someone here to see you. Be quiet as you can. You have ten minutes, I'll come and get you when the taxi's here."

"Okay," said Jimmy, not really understanding as he looked around the room.

"Sally?" He said, once he'd seen. "What are you doing here?"

"I have to talk to you," Sally said, "I have to leave school and go to a new home far away and live with my aunt tomorrow because the school won't let me stay."

Jimmy sat up, rubbing his eyes as Tim let himself out.

"But... when will I see you?" He asked as Sally sat down next to him on the bed.

"I don't know," Sally said shrugging.

"But...but, that's not fair!" Jimmy said, voice rising, making Sally put her fingers to her lips.

"You have to be quiet Jimmy," she said.

"I don't want you to go Sally," Jimmy said, feeling a hole in the pit of his stomach.

"I don't want to go," Sally said. "Maybe you can visit?"

"My mum says I'm not allowed to see you."

"But..."

"But it is okay. In films if you love someone then you find them again and you marry them and it is all okay and you are happy."

"Will that happen with us?"

"I think so."

"Oh. Okay."

"So what do we do now?" Jimmy asked, staring down at his bed sheets.

"I don't know," Sally said. "Will you do hugging like you did at school when we ran away?"

"Okay," Jimmy said, putting his arm around her. And they stayed there, together for what seemed like the last time for them, close as they could be, happy for the moment but looking ahead at a long time apart.

The soft knock seemed to come just a few minutes later, even though Tim had ended up giving them twenty.

"Time to go Sally," he said.

"Okay," Sally said standing up, "bye Jimmy," she said to him.

"Bye Sally," he said standing up. He put his arms around her for one last hug, which both wished would not end. Then they leant back and kissed each other on the lips, feeling not the excitement they felt before, but something more poignant.

That was when the landing light came on.

"What the hell is going on!" Jimmy's mum shouted down the corridor. "Why did I get woken up by a taxi's headlights shining in my room and why are their voices in my house at two in the morning?"

All three froze as the heavy footsteps moved down towards them, then a few seconds later Jimmy's mum, tailed by his dad, appeared in Jimmy's bedroom doorway.

"Sally!" She screeched when she saw her, "What the hell are you doing here?!"

"Look," Tim started, "she's moving away tomorrow, she walked all the way down here just to say good bye to Jimmy, I let her in and now the taxi's here to take her home."

"You're going away?" She asked Sally, her eyes burning. "Good riddance, at least that's something. Now get out of my house. Now!"

"Here you go Sally, give this to the man," Tim said handing her a ten and a five pound note. "I've told him your address."

"Okay. Thank you. Bye Tim. Bye Jimmy," she said quietly. "Bye Mrs Tiffin." She took the money then ran from the room, past Jimmy's parents who stepped aside and down the stairs. Jimmy took one look at everyone in the room, then bolted for the door to follow.

"Where do you think your going?" His mum asked, blocking his way.

"I have to say bye!" He shouted at her. "Let me down now!"

"No way bucko," his mum said shaking her head and putting her hands on his shoulders. "You will stay right here."

"No!" Jimmy shouted at her. "No, no, no! I am going downstairs, I have to, I need to!"

He wriggled out from her grip and bolted out the door, his mum was so surprised she didn't even follow, his Dad could have stopped him but there was something in Jimmy's eyes that made him let him go.

Jimmy made it to the last few stairs then jumped down the rest, landing heavily and loudly in the landing. The door was already opened and he ran straight through, his bare feet landing on sharp stones and other debris that hadn't been cleared from the paved drive.

He could see the taxi, they were already out the drive and getting ready to pull away. He raced out into the road, waving his arms and calling

"Sally! Please!"

But the car got going, moving off just as he was about to get a hand onto it. Now standing in the middle of the road, he realized they weren't going to stop. He jumped up and down, waving still and shouting. He cupped his hands round his mouth and with all his might, waking more then one neighbor he shouted.

"Bye Sally!"

Sally heard, turned around and saw him; and both waved and both felt tears in their eyes as distance began to be put between them, not for the first time. They waved until the taxi, turned the corner and they disappeared from each other's view.

Once he could no longer see the red lights of the car, Jimmy caught his breath and realized he was still in the middle of the road. He breathed deep three times and wiped the tears from his eyes with the sleeve of his top. Then, with one more breath, he turned around and walked back inside.

He felt strange. He knew he was in trouble, knew that his parents were going to shout at him and Tim either now or in the morning, but he didn't care. He felt a pit in his stomach as if some of himself had gone, more empty then ever before, more disappointed then ever before. But still he walked back up the stairs with half a smile that no one but his brother would understand, as he got ready to take his grilling like a man.

College

I

It was five thirty on a Thursday evening, three years and seven months since Sally had moved to her new school. Jimmy and she hadn't seen each other since that night outside his house, but once a week, when his mum was cooking dinner and before his dad got home, they would talk on instant messaging over the internet.

Jimmy was generally happy in the post sixteen department at Hollygroves's; he liked that he went out more through the day, getting to spend loads of time with Robert and Aalap in the community. But it was Thursday evenings he looked forward to with the most zeal, getting to speak to Sally.

He was always online first with the messenger open, staring at the screen, waiting for the picture of her to pop up. And when it did his heart would jump a little. Their conversations took a long time to type but they seemed to fly by:

"Hello Jimmy."
"Hello Sally."

"How are you?"

"I am okay. I watched Enchanted today. It is about a man who gets stabbed in the sleeve but he is okay because it is only his sleeve."

"I have seen it. I thought it was funny with the princess."

"We did cooking today as well. I said that you could make spaghetti and Becky said that was good. She said you could be a cook. Are you going to be a cook?"

"I don't know. Maybe. When I leave school and go to college I will do life skills and cooking and learn how to be a cook."

"But you can cook."

"I need to get certificates."

"Oh."

"How is school?"

"It is okay. Becky does not do hand holding unless we are out in the community."

"Okay."

"How is your aunt's house?"

"It is okay. Me and mum painted my room. It is purple now. We have unpacked all the things in our new flat. My mum has got a job. Does your mum have a job?"

"No."

"Okay."

"How is your mum? Is she still angry?"

"She is a happy now she has a job. I am not doing running away and she is happy about that."

"Good."

"Okay. I have to cook dinner."
"Okay."
"I will message you again soon."
"Okay."
"Bye Jimmy."
"Bye Sally."
"X"

They both signed out and mentally prepared themselves for another week of no contact.

Jimmy took himself upstairs to his room and sat on his bed. He wished he could go and see her, but after the huge blow up that followed the last time they saw each other, he didn't dare suggest it to his mum.

To take his mind off Sally he booted up his PC, Tim's old one that he been given when Tim had been packed off to a London University, and connected up his camera that had been his birthday present all those years ago. He loaded up the movie player and played back the last night's film of his Mum and Dad watching TV and earlier in that evening Aalap, Robert and himself at an after school club they had been to. The shots were mostly of them playing football in the hall and Robert, who was looking more and more adult with his thickening muscles and scratchy beard, showing off his new wrestling moves until one of the support workers stopped him.

The young men on the screen were incomparable to the young men of the year nine class that time ago. Robert had joined the gym in his endless pursuit to be a wrestler and as such had been growing outwards as well as upwards. Aalap had grown a moustache and gotten much taller than anyone Jimmy knew. And Jimmy himself had been growing his hair so he could look more like Captain Jack Sparrow.

Some things hadn't change however. Their dreams remained the same, their school the same and Jimmy was no closer to figuring himself or his disability out. It had become so fruitless asking people, who got embarrassed, changed the subject or threw to many long words at him. He was now looking forward to college to provide more answers.

He watched the footage of the clubs that ran through until the visit he had made with his parents, Robert, Robert's parents and two of Robert's brothers. Aalap was, unfortunately for them, looking at staying at home and going to a local college. Robert and Jimmy were hoping to get places at a residential college called Hayden and were happy to be doing this together, even though they would miss Aalap.

As Jimmy watched the images he'd shot as he walked around the college he felt a mixture of nerves and excitement. It was a huge complex of buildings with accommodation, class rooms, clubs and activities, rugby and football pitches, computer suites and loads of young people and workers. It was a huge change, but as he reminded himself, it's what adults do. Just in the way Tim moved out to go to university, in one year and two months Jimmy was hoping to do the same. He would really be an adult then, he thought as the shots on his camera showed the rooms he'd watch films in, the kitchens he'd cook in and the bedroom he'd call his own; however temporarily.

He'd be a real adult then, away from his parents with his own door key and all. And that was where he'd work out why things were so different for him. Because that's what happens when you're an adult, you begin to understand yourself. Right?

2

Sally was sat outside the post sixteen department of the school she had been forced to leave Hollygroves for, on her lunch break. For the most part she too had had a good few years, making one or two friends, enjoying her lessons, liking the rural grounds and the big parks around the suburbs of her new town.

But things that day weren't so good. In fact they looked like they were due to change.

"I do not think we are girlfriend and boyfriend anymore," She was saying to the quiet George who was sat next to her on a wooden bench.

"But... but I have a girlfriend that is you," George said, playing with the strings that hung from his hoody.

"But... it is that..."

How could she explain to him? She knew that her and Jimmy couldn't be girlfriend and boyfriend since they couldn't see each other, hold hands, hug or kiss like girlfriends and boyfriends did. But similarly she didn't get that same rush with

George that she had with Jimmy and she guessed that was what being in a true relationship was supposed to be. It just wasn't as... something.

"It is that we should not be girlfriend and boyfriend anymore," she said eventually but firmly.

She looked at George who had shrunk, his head was tipped forward and he had tears in his eyes.

"B...B...B...B...but you are my girlfriend. You dumped me. I don't have a g...g...g...g...girlfriend. I have been dumped," he said unhappily.

"Yes," Sally said.

George got up and walked over to his friends on the other side of the playground, hunched over and scuffing his feet as he moved. Once again, Sally was alone. She knew that her friends Becky and Hanna would not talk to her for this, they had told her so, they had been friends with George first. But she couldn't go along with it; she had felt what a true connection felt like.

She was still sad as she watched him go, but more sad because she couldn't have Jimmy than anything else. He was the one for her, she was surer every day, but they were so far away and his mum wouldn't ever let him see her.

Sally felt even more alone half an hour later as she stood in the cooking rooms waiting for her favorite lesson to start; behind her chopped ingredients, selection of plastic bowls, utensils and single gas burner. George had gone back to his old cooking station that he used to share with Sally, but Sally hadn't wanted to join him after everything that had happened so she'd gone to a different one and Becky *had* joined him causing a momentary pang of jealously in Sally. But the crux of it was that Sally now was without anyone to work with and was feeling uncomfortable at her new space.

"Sally, do you not have a partner?" Mr Greenberg asked after everyone had settled, surveying the room of paired up students.

"No," Sally said, shaking her head.

"Perfect. We've got a new student whose joining us today from Oakland and I think you two will get on well. She should be here any moment."

"Okay," Sally said, glad that at least she wouldn't be doing it by herself.

A few moments later and into the room walked a teaching assistant leading by the shoulder a young lady, Sally's age, with blond pigtails tied up with colorful ribbons and wearing a trendy, flowery dress.

"Hi Lilly, welcome to our post sixteen," Mr Greenberg said to the smiling young lady.

"Hello Mr Greenberg I am here to start my lessons now and although Miss Clements is not happy I did not want to hold her hand as I am a seventeen year old lady and I do not need to hold hands," she said in one breath.

"Okay, fair enough," Mr Greenberg said pulling a 'what can you do' smile at the young teachers assistant, who half smiled back before making an exit.

"Class, this is Lilly…"

"Hello!" Said Lilly before Mr Greenberg had got out the rest of his sentence. "My name is Lilly, what is your names?"

"Um… you'll have a chance to get to know them later on. Why don't you join Sally over there for the moment and get to know everyone later?" Mr Greenberg said quickly, averting a cascade of name shouting.

"Okay," Lilly said, "I will go over there now." She moved over, weaving through the tables, looking down at the floor, smiling as broadly as she could. "Hello Sally my name is Lilly are we doing cooking?"

"Yes, we are cooking Curry."

"How do you do cooking curry? Is it good? Curry is spicy."

"Yes."

"Okay. Curry is spicy. Shall we cook some curry?"

"Yes."

"Okay! Let's do cooking!"

"Okay," Sally said, catching Lilly's smile from her and picking up the onion.

After the lesson Lilly stayed close to Sally as they moved through the corridors of the school, back towards their post sixteen class rooms which were at the other end to the cooking rooms. They didn't say much, Lilly was too preoccupied trying to make her eyes meet other eyes all the way along, even when those eyes wouldn't meet hers. At one point she slipped her arm into Sally's arm which made Sally head lift a little higher as they walked. Suddenly it didn't matter much about George anymore, because she wasn't alone, although she was all too aware that these things didn't last.

Later that evening, back at her and her mum's flat, Sally was cooking dinner for herself; alone but happy because her mum was at work earning money rather then spending it at the pub.

Lilly and Sally had swapped numbers before they had left the college and Sally didn't know what to do. She really liked Lilly, she was so full of life, but knew that sometimes people didn't like it when you kept calling them, a lesson she head learnt the hard way from her first ever boyfriend, Bob. She was nervous, was she supposed to not call her, she knew her mum had a lot of numbers in her mobile phone that she didn't call everyday, sometimes even for months. But what if Lilly was angry that Sally hadn't called? What if tomorrow at school she ignored Sally for not calling her? Then she'd be alone again and would have lost the chance to be friends with one of the nicest people she'd ever met!

Sally was getting so worked up she forgot to turn down the heat on the oven so her shepherds pie burnt and she only noticed when smoke started pouring out. In her rush to get it out she then forgot to slip on the oven gloves, burning herself and dropping the dish on the floor where it smashed on impact.

"Argh!" She screamed and ran to the sink to run her hand under the tap like they had shown her at school. Just then, her phone rang.

"Hello?" She said, picking it up with her less sore hand.

"Hello Sally this is Lilly from your class at College you gave me your number so I thought I would call you to see how you are and what you are doing?"

"I am burning my hand and I dropped the dish and it broke."

"Oh dear, that is a shame, we are about to have dinner here, would you like to have dinner with us today, I asked my mum and she said she could come and pick you up from your home if it isn't too far but I think it is not to far as we both get buses home and the buses are all near by?"

"Yes. My dinner is in the bin."

"Okay, what is your address and my mum can put it in her Sat-Nav map in the car."

"It is Flat 19, Elmwood Crescent."

"Okay, I will see you in a bit, bye Sally."

The phone went dead and Sally smiled to herself as she got the dust pan and brush out the cupboard under the sink, hand still throbbing, but she didn't care too much.

This is what friends do, she thought to herself. *I have a friend now!*

3

Jimmy was sat between Aalap and Robert in the midst of their leaver's assembly another year on from when he had told Sally about Enchanted. He was nervous, it was his last day in Hollygroves's and although Robert would be coming with him, College was a daunting prospect. He'd already stayed in the residential placement at 'Hayden' for two nights and three days for his assessment so he kind of knew what to expect, but there was a big difference between two nights and living there. He would come home one weekend a month to see his family, all of whom were sitting in the rows for parents at the back of the sports hall. Even Tim had come back from University for this. The sixth form leavers were all sitting at the front and now that they had done the hymns, it was time for them to take turns to collect their certificates.

There was classical music playing over the ceremony and the hall had been decorated in preparation for the day with banners and pictures up around the walls. There was electricity in the air as each of the young people in Jimmy's year looked ahead, if they could, at the prospects that had been laid before them. Out of the eight leavers, seven were going to residential colleges like Jimmy and only Aalap was going to a local college that he would access along with the more able young people from Glen Park, Sally's old school. None were going into work, none were aware of the option.

One by one their names were called and they walked, or were pushed in their wheelchairs, up to the front where they were handed a folder with the certificates that they'd worked towards. Meaningful certificates but not that powerful when it would come to looking for jobs.

When Jimmy's name was called he went up and shook Mrs Dorite's hand and she handed him his folder. He then turned, as instructed, so that his mum, who had moved into the aisle, could take a picture. Everyone was smiling and clapping him and it felt good, just like if he had won an Oscar.

After they had all been up the teachers played a power point show consisting of more pictures of the sixth form college and the things that they had done. Jimmy watched as past memories floated before him and when he turned around he noticed that his mum had started to cry.

Later that evening Jimmy, Aalap and Robert were getting ready for their leavers prom at Jimmy's house up in his room, radio tuned into Radio 1 and turned up loud. Each of them had hired a suit for the occasion and after spraying deodorant so thick they coughed, they got dressed, combed and gelled their hair, applied aftershave on top of the deodorant and went downstairs to wait.

Robert picked up the bunch of flowers that he had bought earlier with the help of his brother and sat with them in his lap, watching out the window for their ride.

The Limo picked them up at seven thirty and after being arranged for photos by Jimmy's still tearful mum, they climbed inside.

"Let's get going!" Robert said helping himself to a coke out of the fridge. "This is awesome dudes!" He added, putting his arms around his two best mates.

"Yes dudes this is awesome." Aalap said. "I'm wearing a suit actually. That is very grown up."

"Yes, we are very smart," said Jimmy who wished his mum had let him take his video camera with him. "We are being adults now. Let's go do a party!"

The limo pulled up outside the church hall and they got out, one by one and stood together for a moment before the party with the music that they could hear through the walls. The place was vibrating, they could feel it, they could feel the excitement in the air. This was it, their last night as children before they made the first steps into adulthood. Even the activities Jimmy was going to over the summer were run by adult services rather than children's. He'd be going to the nineteen and over group now.

They each took a moment, took a breath and then together walked into the entrance where Miss Fields was sitting behind a plastic table, wearing a long dress.

"Hello lads," she said, scanning her eyes down the list in front of her and ticking off the three boys.

"Hello Julie," Robert said, offering his hand which she took. He moved her hand up to his lips and brushed them against her knuckles. After all, she wasn't his teacher anymore. Miss Fields blushed and quickly moved her hand to her side.

"Through there lads," she said pointing to the main hall.

"Okay Julie. Thank you. We will go do partying now," Aalap said with a grin.

"S...S...Sarah here?" Robert asked with a rare stutter.

"Yes, I think so."

"Okay. She is my date."

"I know Robert, you said today."

"She is my date for the party."

"Yes Robert, she'll be in there with the others," Miss Fields said, nodding towards the halls entrance.

The church hall had been decked out for a proper party and was over three quarters full of sixth form students spanning over three years and staff. A DJ was playing good music which the young adults were bopping to and waving a rubber chicken about which was largely ignored. Tables of food were set up around one corner and the hatch was serving drinks. Everyone over eighteen had been allowed one beer token each, a gesture to signify adulthood that had had to be signed off by their parents earlier on in the month.

"Sarah," Robert said, noticing his date hovering about by the food tables along with Di and Jane, other young people in their sixth form. He headed over and in front of everyone gave her a bow and handed over the pink and purple bouquet, much to her embarrassed delight. She took them and sniffed them, then held out her hand which he took and pulled her to him, slipping an arm around her waist and taking her other hand in his so they could awkwardly waltz to the Hip Hop, her still with the flowers in hand. Aalap was watching with a measure of jealously, Robert was fast becoming a confident man; he just seemed to know what to do, unlike Aalap who was unsure what to even say to a girl.

Aalap and Jimmy left them to it and went to speak to a group of friends who had moved up to the post sixteen department that year. After they'd said hi they went to exchange their vouchers for beers so they could make it into a proper party.

A few weeks ago had been Jimmy's younger brother Sam's prom party and Sam had regaled Tim, who had come down to visit, and Jimmy with tales of sneaking alcohol, chatting up girls and riding in limousines. Of course they didn't have to have the support workers, something Jimmy and his friends were all too aware of, but they did have a lot of teachers that had turned up, so that was pretty similar. As he took his beer and stood watching the dancing young people, although so many things were different for him; for example some people at his prom needed help to dance, like Sophie who was smiling and giggling and waving her arms up and down in pleasure as Miss Gordon pushed her around in her wheelchair, he couldn't help but feel that this was how it should be. This was being a young adult.

The night wore on, Robert's date got angry with him for dancing with her friend and so he came over to his mates who were sitting at the side of the hall amongst friends. Jimmy got up to go and get a drink and saw that Charlie was sitting by himself on the other side of the hall. He was still angry with him for making Sally so upset and for lying, but he went over anyway.

"Hello Charlie," he said and put his hand out.

"Hello Jimmy my old mate," Charlie said and took his hand in his. Jimmy smiled and went back on his way to get himself a coke, feeling even more of a man, tying one more loose end up.

At the end of the night the DJ played a slower song and all the young couples danced. Robert and Sarah had made up and were holding each other close and a couple of the teachers started crying, which Jimmy didn't understand since *they* weren't the ones leaving. But as he watched all the people he had known for so long dance, especially standing next to Aalap who he wouldn't see for months at a time, he felt himself well up a bit too. So he wiped his eyes, smiled as broadly as he could and sang along to the words he had heard so many times before on the radio.

4

Sally was feeling good. Earlier on that day Lilly and her mum, Teresa, had dyed a purple streak into Sally's hair and cut it shorter then she was used to. 'Just like a pop star,' Lilly had kept saying. She was wearing new clothes that her and her mum had got in the town and she felt positively like a new woman. And here they were, two young ladies together, about to go and do what most young ladies do. Spend an evening with friends, albeit ones they hadn't met yet, at a social event with a bar.

"Have a great time girls!" Teresa said through the open car window. "Now are you sure you don't need me to go in with you?"

"No thank you Mum we will go in and do signing in and if there is a problem we will give you a call on the mobile phones that we have and then you can come pick us up," Lilly said catching her mum's eye.

"Okay then," Teresa said smiling her sweet smile. "And your mum is picking up at 9, yes Sally?"

"Yes."

"Okay then, enjoy!"

"Okay," Sally said. "Bye."

"See you later," she said then drove off.

"Come on Sally. Let's go do signing in," Lilly said, slipping her am in Sally's.

They walked together towards the entrance of the bowling ally. Both were clutching the letters they had been sent about this 'special needs activity' and both were interested in bowling. After they saw Teresa drive by waving however, Lilly stopped to pull out a packet of cigarettes that she'd had some trouble buying earlier from a man who couldn't seem to understand what she was asking for:

"Does your carer know you're here?" He had asked. "Why not come back with your mum?" That one stung.

"I am nineteen years old," Lilly had stammered out. "Here is my identification please may I have twenty cigarettes."

"I don't think so young lady," he had said.

"Why not?"

"Because...."

"You can buy and smoke cigarettes from eighteen years old and I am nineteen years old. I am an adult and I live with my mum but I am going to move out soon and be in a house and get support to cook and do cleaning and I am going to have a job."

The man looked at her for some time before finally taking her money, certain that at some point he'd have an irate dad screaming at him like he sometimes did when he let some of the younger girls and guys purchase alcohol or smokes.

Lilly waited before her mum was well out of sight before she lit a cigarette and the two of them went and stood by the entrance.

"Sally, would you like to have a cigarette?" She asked, but Sally shook her head. Her mum smoked and she hated the way the smell clung to her clothes and stuck to her hair. Somehow Lilly just smelled of the lilac perfume that she bought by the gallon.

Once Lilly had let the end of the cigarette drop from her fingers and crushed it beneath her shoe, the two of them went inside and walked up to the reception desk.

"We are here for special needs activities," Lilly said. Sally liked that she would do all the talking.

"Okay," said the tanned, handsome man behind the desk. "It's at the end; lane numbers one, two and three."

They both turned to where he was pointing and saw a large group of people ranging from about nineteen to sixty standing around holding drinks and chatting.

They walked over to the group and instinctively went to the person with the clipboard.

"Hi there we are Sally and Lilly and are here for the special needs bowling activity," Lilly said to the man.

"Welcome!" He said to them. "My name's Michael and I organize the event. Bowling will start in fifteen minutes and you are both on lane three with four other adults. The bar is over there, you're more then welcome to have a drink while we wait for everything to be ready and I can then introduce you to your team mates. Have you both paid for this?"

"No," said Sally, reaching into her back pocket. "Here you go," she said handing over the twenty pound note, feeling grown up and responsible.

"Is this for you both?" Mike asked.

"I don't know."

"I have money too for the activity," said Lilly

"Then I guess its not. Here you go Sally," Mike said handing her fifteen pounds change and taking Lilly's ten pound note.

"Shall we get a drink?" Lilly asked Sally.

"Okay," Sally said, pocketing her change.

They went to the bar together, Lilly's arm still linked in Sally's. The whole area was pretty empty apart from a few older men in one corner, drinking pints and staring wordlessly at a football game, but it was still pretty exiting for the girls who'd never been in an area like this without supervision before. They had to wait a few minutes while the barman put away a stack of glasses, before he wandered listlessly over.

"Can I have a drink please?" Sally asked the barman.

"What would you like?"

"Um, a coke with alcohol please," she said, not knowing the name of the stuff her mum sometimes added to coke at home.

"A vodka coke?" The barman asked.

Sally turned round to see Mike talking to other people.

"I think a...a vodka and coke," Sally said, stammering just a little, having seen an advert on the dangers of Vodka just recently.

"You sure?" He asked.

"Yes she is," Lilly said. "And we are nineteen years old and have identification so we are allowed to have alcoholic drinks."

"I'm sure you are," the barman said with a slight sigh. He turned round and poured Sally's drink, the first she'd ever bought.

"Three pounds," he said to Sally, who handed him the change she'd just been given. He looked at it, gave her the ten pound note back and ran the drink through the till before giving her a further two pound coins and a receipt.

"And for you?" He asked Lilly.

"I will also have a vodka and coke because I am nineteen and I have identification," she said. The barman sighed again and went to pour the drink.

Back at the lanes they were introduced to their team mates, two lads in their early twenties, a woman around thirty and a man of about forty.

Sally was pleased that there were young men there, not so happy about the others, but could live with it, she thought, as she shook each of their hands. Then, all that was left to do was to type their names into the computer and start the games.

At first Sally stayed with Lilly, sitting together on the interlinked plastic chairs on the side, sipping their drinks slowly at first then draining them pretty quick. By their third drink she plucked up her courage and went to chat.

"Do you like doing bowling Paul?" She asked one of the lads who was doing his best to carry a bowling ball, with fingers that didn't work too well.

"Yes. But it is quite hard."

"Oh."

"But it is good to see my best friend Sammy S who is over there on the chair." He pointed to Sammy who gave the girls a three fingered wave.

"Come on Paul," the thirty something lady said with an exaggerated sigh.

"Okay, okay, okay calm down, calm down," Paul said smiling at the girls and shaking his head. "Here I go then."

Sally watched him awkwardly amble to the line where he threw it as hard as he could in the direction of the pins. It bounced a few times off the barriers and only knocked over a couple of them. Paul watched it until the end and then flicked his long, straw colored hair back, smiled and wandered back over to get another ball.

After his turn was over, he wandered back to the girls.

"It is now my best friend's turn. Sammy S. He is going to go next," Paul said motioning to Sammy who got up to take his turn. "So is this your first time here?"

"Of course it is," the older lady whose name was Julie said with another sigh. "Otherwise you would have seen them before, wouldn't you?"

"Yes, you're right actually," Paul said brightly. "I guess that's true, I would have seen you before as I always come here. Well spotted."

"Yes it is our first time. When we became nineteen we went to adult services, not children's services and they said we could come do bowling and we said we would like to come as we like bowling, didn't we Sally?"

"Yes we did," Sally said smiling.

"Yes, I know adult services actually. We do a lot of things with them like activities."

"Yes, activities are good. They are very, very good!" Sammy said, having thrown his second ball and fancying a conversation.

"Yes. Did you do well?" Paul asked.

"Yes, I did very well."

"Did you get a strike?"

"Yes, I got a strike!"

"No you didn't," said Julie pointedly wagging her finger at him. "You got six pins."

"Oh. I did not get a strike," Sammy said shrugging. "Should we all go and get a drink?"

"Yes, we should go and get a drink," Lilly said coyly.

A few more goes and Julie was getting more and more frustrated with her younger team mates as they spent more time chatting and less time playing. The other two lanes were taking it all that much more seriously, especially on the one next to them where each competitor was ready to go with their ball just as the one before them got to the line. There was little talking on those lanes and both Lilly and Sally guessed rightly that Julie would have rather have been with them. It got to the point where Michael, the guy in charge, asked them nicely if they'd like to forego the next game and go and sit in the bar where they could chat or play pool, only if they weren't interested in playing. All four of them jumped at this, not just for the opportunity to get away from Julie's constant moaning, but also the rarity of doing something outside an organized activity. Sure the support workers and Michael would still be there, watching them, checking up on them but they would at least be aside from the group, doing their own thing on their own time.

The bar was busier then it had been at first, with a few groups of late teens, laughing and flirting loudly, congregating round the pool table, the dart board or the computerized quiz machine. Most of the groups had had a few to drink and they were all too self involved to even notice the four as anything other than another group of teenagers; even with Paul's clumsy movements. They each got another drink and took a table in view of the bowling, away from the noisy, flashing fruit machines and far enough away from the group to feel separate.

"So do you do working or college?" Lilly asked the lads.

"College. At Hayden, it is where we used to sleep," Sammy S answered. "Now we have a house in the town."

"It is good there. We have been there one year," Paul said.

"Oh, okay," said Sally nodding, trying to place the name of the college and who it was who had mentioned it before. "Is Julie always grumpy?"

"Yes, yes, she is grumpy!" Sammy S said laughing.

"Okay, now here's the big one," Paul said, smiling and looking away. "The big question! Could we have your numbers so that one day we could meet up with you again soon? That's the biiiig question!"

"Yes, that would be okay!" Lilly said, blushing now.

"Okay," said Sally getting out her phone. "I can put your number in here?"

"Okay!" Said Sammy S, waving his arms up and down in excitement. "That's okay, to be honest!"

They all stayed in their booth, sipping drinks slowly, until Sally's mum called to let them know she was in the car park. The girls wandered out to meet her on shaky legs.

"Hello Mrs Hummel!" Lilly exclaimed loudly as Sally struggled to open the car door, finally managing it but opening it to hard, making her step backwards, trip on the curb and land on her bum on the pavement. "How are you?" Lilly asked as she helped Sally stand and move into the car.

Sally's mum didn't reply, just pulled her lips in thin and waited until they were settled. She didn't say a word in fact until she'd dropped Lilly off at her home and her and Sally were getting out the car and walking up the path to their flat.

"Your drunk, aren't you Sally? What did I say about drinking? You can't go about acting irresponsibly like that, otherwise you won't be able to go out. Do you hear me Sally? Sometimes I just don't know what to do with you, you know that? Sometimes I wonder…"

"I am nineteen years old and I have identification and I am allowed to have alcoholic drinks!" Sally shouted at her mum as they stepped into the hall, before she ran clumsily up the stairs and shut the door to her room, where she threw herself onto her bed and lay for several minutes, smiling, shaking and laughing.

5

Every now and then Jimmy would look out the window. He didn't do this much, he didn't like how everything flashed by too quickly without time to take in the whole picture. But every now and then he'd try, just to see the landscape change, shops becoming houses, then the buildings becoming sparser; becoming fields… they were going a long way out into the sticks.

He shifted the suitcase on his lap but still couldn't make it comfortable. Yet he felt more secure holding a load of his things to him.

As they pulled into the entrance of his new college, his stomach back flipped and shivers ran through his whole body. A mixture of nerves and excitement took over as they navigated their way through the long, speed bumped roads to reach the car park and the reception desk. When they'd parked up his mum, in the passenger seat of the car, started crying again, so his Dad and him didn't move until she was ready.

They went into the main building and went up to reception where they signed themselves in and collected visitors badges.

"You must be the Tiffins!" A chirpy voice called to them. They turned around and were greeted by a large smile from the most colorfully dressed lady Jimmy had ever seen. Her purple leopard skin print skirt and lime green cardigan stood out amongst the white walls of the college. "And you must be Jimmy," she said extending a hand to him, "I'm Polly. How was your trip?"

"Okay," Jimmy said.

"Well, it's nice to see you're here so early. Come on; let's get you settled in shall we? If you take your car round to the accommodation I'll show you your room. I'm the head support worker for you Jimmy and you'll be sharing with six others."

"Is Robert here yet?" Jimmy asked.

"Nope, you're the first. You two went to the same school, didn't you?"

"Yes."

"Well, always nice to have a familiar face isn't it?"

"Yes."

"Well I'm sure he'll come later," she said. "So I'll meet you by the accommodation?"

"We'll be there in a minute," Jimmy's dad said nodding.

Jimmy's parents left a few hours later. His mum had wanted to stay and help him sort his things out, but he was eager to make it his own so had only let them set up his television and the rack for his DVDs and videos. When they left his Dad had given him a handshake and had said:

"You're an adult now son." Which made him feel so grown up.

His mum had cried again and hugged him for a long time and told him to ring her if he ever needed anything, which he promised to do. Then they left, and he was all on his own.

Though he wasn't all on his own. He had Polly who kept popping in to check if he was okay and he'd soon have Robert. To keep himself busy he started to organize his room, putting his DVDs in order and putting all his clothes away in drawers and on hangers in his wardrobe.

He'd been so engrossed in putting up pictures in the right way; he barely heard the voice at his door.

"Jimmy?" Polly called.

"Yes," Jimmy said.

"May I come in?"

"Yes."

She opened the door and stuck her head through the gap, her hoop earrings jangling together as she did.

"Everyone's here now mate, we thought we'd have a meeting in the kitchen if you'd like?"

"Okay," Jimmy said.

He followed her out into the corridor, down past many white doors like his and into the kitchen where around the table sat five other boys, one of whom beamed as soon as he saw him. Robert had arrived without him knowing, while he'd been unpacking. He smiled back and went and took the empty chair that was next to him.

"Right then," Polly said, "let's start with introductions. How about we go around the table and each say our name and our favorite thing? It could be a hobby maybe or an item. For instance, my name is Polly and I love going to the cinema. How about you go?" She said motioning to the lad next to her who had thick glasses and a cap on.

"I am Ben. I like football," he said.

"My name is Zack," said the next lad. "I like shopping for shoes, like brown ones or black ones."

"My name is Robert and I loooovvveee wrestling and beautiful women!" Robert said laughing.

"I'm Jimmy. And I love films and I am going to do work with films when I'm older," Jimmy said.

"Adam," said the next guy looking down at the table and shaking slightly. "Watching cars."

"My name's Phillip and I love Eastenders," said the last.

"Well okay then guys. Here's the plan. Tonight, for all those who are interested, we thought we'd have some dinner and then head out to a get to know you event they're holding in the hall here. Then tomorrow we'll have an orientation around the college. How does that sound for a plan?"

"Great!" Robert said.

"Excellent. What do you guys fancy for dinner? Normally we'd have to shoot down to the shops and get the food, but today we thought sod it, lets get take out."

"Pizza!" Robert said quickly.

"Okay, what about the rest of you?"

"Pizza is good," Jimmy said

"Yeah, pizza," Zack said, "pizza is the best like pepperoni, or pineapple, or ham or mushrooms, or sweet corn, or tomatoes, no olives, or onion..."

"Okay with everyone?" Polly quickly interjected, looking at the others who nodded. "Pizza it is then."

"I have a question," said Jimmy, unsure whether or not to put his hand up.

"Okay, what's up?"

"Um... the ceiling is up?" Jimmy asked, wrinkling his nose, confused.

"Sorry, I mean what's your question?" Polly asked suppressing a giggle.

"When do we get keys for our room? Adults have keys for their room?"

"I'm not sure they have keys, these doors," Polly said. "But we can ask the head teacher if you like?"

"But adults have keys? I thought we were doing being an adult?"

"I don't know, we'll ask," Polly said.

"Okay," said Jimmy un-convinced, "but if I'm going to do being an adult, I need a key."

"Yeah!" said Robert.

"Okay guys, we'll ask," Polly said. "Now let's go get ready for this get to know you event!"

After they'd eaten and cleared the boxes from the kitchen, Jimmy went to his room to change. Sitting on the bed that he couldn't quite see as his own, he put in one of the videos that he'd lined up next to the family's old TV that he'd been donated;

newer then the one Tim had got, but half the size of the one he'd got used to at home.

He fast forwarded Die Hard to his favorite scene when Bruce Willis puts the bad guy in the lift with the sign around his neck and watched this over and over, nineteen times before the knock came at his door, an un-familiar sound that made this room even more alien.

Not knowing how to answer, Jimmy rewound the thirty nine seconds of footage and watched it again, turning the sound up a few green bars on the box. Half way through the second time round since the knock, it came again.

"Heelllloooooooo Jimmy! It's Robert! You in there?"

"Yes," Jimmy called back.

"Can I come in as well?"

"Yes," said Jimmy.

The door swung open and Robert came in, having dolled himself up with a white shirt with the collar turned up and black shoes.

"What's that smell?" Jimmy asked smiling.

"It is deodorant."

"You have put a lot on."

"The ladieess love deodorant. I'm going on the p..prowl tonight."

"Oh, okay then. Should I wear a shirt?"

"You need to wear a shirt, the ladies love a shirt."

"Oh, okay. Then I will wear a shirt. Where do I get a shirt?"

"I'll give you a shirt!"

"Okay."

"Follow me mate," Robert said and led the way out of Jimmy's room.

6

"Hello Sally," Jimmy typed into his computer.

"Hello Jimmy. How are you?" Came the reply in a pretty, cursive font.

"Why is your words pink now?" He typed back.

"Lilly made me change it. She said pink is more me," Sally said, smiling to herself.

"Oh. Okay."

"Lilly is my best friend. We do everything together. On the other day we went to Sammy S's and Paul's supported living house. It is very nice."

"Oh," said Jimmy feeling a pang of envy in his gut.

"They are very nice. I think you would like them very much."

"Okay," said Jimmy, not feeling any better about Sammy S and Paul.

"We watched a film called 'Anchor Man.' It is very funny when they all have a fight and there are fires and a fork gets thrown."

"Okay."

"How is College?"

"College is okay. My room is very nice. We had a party on Monday and there were a lot of people and I was very glad that Robert was there. He kissed three girls because he wore a lot of deodorant and a shirt. I wore a shirt but did not do kissing. I watch films in my room or in the lounge. We cook food but we are not as good as you are at doing cooking. We cooked pasta but the water went and the pasta burned."

"Oh. You need to have a lot of water."

"Okay."

"It becomes steam."

"I have friends at College. Next week we are going to another college to do a course. It is a mainstream college. I have joined a film club as well."

"That is good. Will they teach you to be a film man?"

"I think so. And then I can go do work in films when College is finished."

"I have a social worker who will help me do living with support workers when I have finished college which starts tomorrow."

"That is good. What is that?"

"It means I live with my friends."

"Okay."

"Yes."

"Would I do that?"

"I think so."

"Okay. Then I would live with Robert."

"Yes. I will live with Lilly. Maybe where we used to live. Mum says she can get a job there now and then we could go back."

"Okay."

"I have to go."

"Okay."

"Speak on Thursday."

"Okay."

"☺"

"x"

"XX"

Jimmy waited until Sally's profile said 'offline' before he went to join his flat mates for their dinner.

7

Sally's alarm sounded at 6:45am, but she was already awake, staring up at her ceiling, watching the way dawn crept across it as the sun rose outside her window.

"Lilly will be there," She whispered to herself in the gloom.

"But what if she makes other friends and then forgets me?"

"No, she is your best friend. She will not do that."

"But what if she does?"

She shook her head and got out of bed, folded back her blue duvet and went downstairs, Sammy the cat behind her, to make herself a cup of tea. Today was the first day of her new full time course at a mainstream college within the town.

Her mum was already downstairs, sitting with a cup of tea at the kitchen table, wearing her work smock over a white blouse. She smiled as Sally came in, but it was a weary smile since she'd been to the pub last night.

"You ready to go?" She asked.

"Yes. I need to do packing my bag. Lilly is coming over then we are going to get the bus."

"Okay," her mum said, making a move as if to hug her, but stopped herself short, "Sally, I hope you know… I hope you know I found it hard when your dad left."

"Yes."

"And that I'm happier up here, away from all the things that reminded me of him."

"Yes, you smile more."

"Yes, yes I do," she said, smiling now. "Okay, I gotta go to work, enjoy your day and we'll go out for pizza this evening to celebrate."

"Okay then," Sally said, wondering why her mum's eyes seemed to be watering.

Sally was sat having her second cup of tea when Lilly rang the doorbell. She was about fifteen minutes early which sent Sally into a moment's panic.

She opened the door and her friend was there, dressed in a pleated black skirt and a bright green hooded top.

"Hello Sally, are you ready to do traveling by buses to go to College?"

"Yes," Sally said, really wanting to go finish her tea and brush her teeth again. "I will get my bag. You look very pretty."

"So do you, I like your pink top and your purple bit in your hair still looks very cool."

"Thank you."

The bus journey took about fifteen minutes; they got off outside the College and stepped out onto the pavement. Both girls stopped dead and looked across the full, vast car park; filled even at ten past nine with milling students, smoking, laughing, slapping each other's backs or hands. The noise and the lack of structure about the whole scene made both girls anxious, all Sally wanted to do was turn and run, rather then risk forcing her way over the minefield before them, but Lilly had never run from anything and that was not going to change. She casually pulled out a cigarette and tried to light it with trembling hands that couldn't get the flick of the wheel right. She tried over and over as Sally watched, getting more and more nervous, knowing this wasn't cool, knowing that the others wouldn't have had a problem with this.

"Hey!" Came a call from two punky girls with lip piercings who'd got off the bus after them.

'Hey' both girls thought struggling to get to grips with the word. Hey, wasn't that an angry word? Or like, as in horse? Or as in, stop that!?

"You need a light?" One asked, stepping forward, brandishing a lighter. Lilly, too nervous and hating herself for being so struggled to say:

"My cigarette is not lit," stuttering a bit as she did.

"Yep, that's why I said did you need to borrow a lighter," the pink haired one said, pulling a face.

"Yes please," Lilly said, allowing the girl to produce a flame that she then lit her cigarette from.

"This you girls' first day?"

"Yes it is," Lilly said feeling better having got the cigarette going, "We are college students and it is our first day and we are Sally and Lilly and we are nineteen."

"That's cool," the pink haired one said smiling at her friend. "Well I'm Penny, and this is Amber. You guys are doing that, what's it course. Right? Up in the building at the end?"

"We...we...we... are college students come to do work," Lilly said, cursing inwardly at every tripped over word.

"We need to go to our lessons now," Sally said, taking her friend's arm. "We will see you soon."

"Right then girls, enjoy!" Penny said grinning widely. "We'll see you around."

Sally pulled Lilly away from the girls and into the car park mine field, keeping her head down as she did, weaving in and out of cars and people; most of whom moved to let them through, some who didn't.

By the time they'd got into reception they were both exhausted and collapsed on the soft blue chairs by the reception desk, breathing hard.

"Can I help you guys?" A soft voice asked from the reception window.

"We are college students. It is our first day."

"Okay, are you skills for life girls then?" The receptionist asked now speaking clearer and more pronounced.

"Yes, that is our course at the college."

"Okay, I'll call someone up to come get you."

"Okay. Is that for new students?" said Sally.

"Not all students, just those who need some extra help."

Once again she thought of Jimmy. He so wanted to understand why he was different and so, she guessed, did she. Why couldn't she be trusted to find the room herself? After all, they'd got here by themselves and made it across the car park themselves. But she was too tired to question so she sat back and waited for their escort.

The skills for life provision was at the far end of the college grounds and took up one of the college's four buildings. Their escort, who'd walked between them the whole way up, through the long corridors and past the mainstream classrooms, led them into a room that was one of the two classrooms for the skills for working life group.

"He...he...hello girls!" A familiar voice called as they entered the room. Sammy C and Paul were sat at the front of the room, looking out at the class of new students who'd assembled themselves around desks.

"Sammy C! Paul!" Lilly called. "Do you also go to this college where we have just started?"

"Why yes we do! We do go to this college to be honest. We are in the last year and today we are doing helping new students," Sammy C said.

"Paul and Sammy, you guys are actually students over at the residential college aren't you?" A nearby support worker clarified. "But they have been taking courses here for three years so they're more than qualified to show you all around."

"Good," said Sally, happy to see such friendly faces,

"Yes it is!" Said Sammy C, then remembering his job added: "Please do take a seat where there is a seat and we will do a talk when everyone is here."

"Okay," Sally said and they went to sit down.

From there, the day just got better. Sammy C and Paul showed them round the college, pointing out the different classrooms for the other students, the canteen and the outside areas for eating or smoking. The girls enjoyed being with the lads who moved around the college with such confidence and ease, smiling at all the other students, whether they smiled back or not.

At one strange point, Sally could have sworn she saw Jimmy come in with another group of young people with disabilities, but she wrote it off as her imagination. After all, he was doing his residential school and she was doing her college course. And on top of that the man she saw had long hair

Jimmy doesn't have long hair, she told herself.

8

"But when do we do film making?" Jimmy asked the teacher who was trying to take control of the proceedings at his college.

Robert and him had signed up to the film club and were sitting in a classroom after their standard lessons had finished, in front of a projector that the teacher had set up. Both had wrongly assumed that the film club would be tutorials in how to make films.

"We don't Jim, we watch films."

"But I thought I was going to learn how to do working in films?"

"Look, we don't even have a camera."

"I have a camera!" Jimmy said, holding his well worn camera high so they could all see. "I make films of my friends and family and activities and when I am older someone will tell me what to film and I will film it and then I will work in films."

"Okay, good luck with that."

"But I watch films in my room or in our lounge. That is where we do watching films."

"Jimmy, this is what it is, no different!" the teacher said. "Now lets…"

"Okay. But why do we watch films together when we can watch it on my own?" Jimmy asked, ignoring the attempt by the teacher to move on.

"That is a good point actually," a man Jimmy hadn't met before said from where he was sat near the back.

"Yes," Robert said. "Jimmy is very good at films! He is going to be a film man!"

"Is he?" Said the young man who spoke up before.

"Look, guys this is a film club for people who want to watch films on the projector, like going to the cinema," the teacher said. "If you don't want to stay, you don't have to stay."

"Then I will go," Jimmy said.

"Me too!" Robert said.

"And me as well actually," Paul said from the back .

They all headed out into the corridor and the others in the group settled down to watch their films.

****

"Polly?" Jimmy asked, quickening his stride so he could walk next to his house tutor as they made their way into town to buy their dinner, later on that day. "Where do you go to learn how to do films?"

"Most people do it at college, or university mate," said Polly, distracted by the pub window they were passing.

"Okay so I am at college, where do I go?"

"Um, sorry Jimmy, apart from the film club at ours, there's nowhere to go."

"But you said do it at college?" Robert said, breaking off his conversation with his latest crush from the accommodation next to theirs, who was joining them on their walk into town.

"But yes... well, they do. But not special colleges like ours. At special colleges like ours, you learn how to live in society. Like how to use money or buses or make tea and coffee. Do you remember that college we looked around the other week? The mainstream college in town? You can do it there."

"Can I do it there?"

"No mate. Our deal with the college is you can do cooking or design technology there."

"Okay, so that means I can't do film?" Jimmy asked, not even trying to hide his disappointment. "Is it because I have autism?"

"Yes, I guess so," Polly said, feeling on safer grounds.

"So what does autism mean?" Jimmy asked, exasperated.

"Well Jimmy, it means you find things hard. So people with Autism need help to use buses and money and talking to people..."

"But Zack has autism and he knows every bus. And my friend Aalap knows how to use money and wait for change and Robert talks to every one..."

"Yes, but Robert has Down's syndrome."

"Yes, but then he could do talking and Zack could do buses and we could do helping each other. And if everyone who has autism needs help on buses then why does Zack not need help on buses but he still has help on buses, like when he knows the three buses to go to town and he can do it but he needs a support worker…"

"For just in case," Polly answered quickly, "now where…"

"For just in cases what?"

"Because it's the way it is," Polly snapped, "if you want to be normal then you need help and what if Zack gets hurt?"

"What if *you* use buses and get hurt?"

"Well… well… well I don't have an excuse of a disability. Now drop it Jimmy and just accept it," she said, quickening her step so she moved on ahead of him and the group, her skirt swishing around her ankles as she moved.

"I don't understand," he said turning to Robert.

"Forget it dude! Look, is that Sally?" He asked pointing in a cafe window.

Jimmy glanced over and saw the girl he'd noticed before in the college they visited, the one who did look a bit like Sally and although Jimmy wouldn't like to admit it, was possibly even prettier then Sally.

"No. Sally is not in this place. And Sally has long hair. And no purple in her hair," he told Robert, keeping his eyes on the girl until they were well out of sight. "Where is Rachel?"

"Here I am!" Said Rachel, coming up beside them and taking Roberts hand.

"You have a girlfriend now?" Jimmy asked.

"No," said Robert quickly, to Rachel's obvious disappointment, "I am not ready to settle dude! And when I am a wrestler I will have to travel everywhere and it will be hard to have a girlfriend."

"Oh. Are we not going to do living with support when we have finished school, like the man talked about?"

"Yes dude!" Robert said. "But that will be my home. I will go there when I am not kicking some ass in the ring like undertaker!"

"Oh. Okay then," said Jimmy, looking ahead to see if he could spot the shops yet.

"Are you looking forward to the party next week? There's going to be loads of ladies!"

"Yes," said Jimmy, looking down. "But there is only one lady I want."

"It's going to rock on!" Robert added, punching the air for effect.

After they'd got back, cooked and eaten, all six of Jimmy's flat mates went and sat in the common room, Jimmy with his camera on his lap, Robert and Zack playing pool. Jimmy, so disappointed with the day, was looking back through past memories and feeling nostalgic. That thought cloud he'd filled in, what seemed like many lifetimes ago now, still had prominence in his head. Work in films. Get married and live in a house. Sorted.

Then why did his dreams seem so out of reach?

"Are you okay?" Robert asked, having potted the black and wandered over to Jimmy.

"No," Jimmy told his friend. "They said on the open day that we would be adults here. My dad said I was an adult. But adults do work. And they will not let me do work. And adults have wives and Sally is not here. And adults have a key to their rooms. And we do not have keys to our rooms. We are not adults."

"Yeah, i...it is right," Robert said, sitting down on the bean bag next to his friend. "Should we go and do asking about the door key? Make you happy?"

"I want to be an adult. I want to do what other adults do. And I want to know why I cannot be now because of autism!" Jimmy said, eyes burning a little fueled by frustration and anxiety.

"Okay," said Robert patting Jimmy on his shoulder. "We will be adults soon and you will work in films."

"How do you know?"

"Because you are great at films. And if you are very good then you should work with them!"

"Okay," said Jimmy turning his eyes back to the camera. "Let's go do asking for door keys."

9

Jimmy was ready for a fight. He had Robert and Zack either side of him and was being shown the way by a reluctant Polly who'd assumed they were going to forget about what she'd said. She was wrong.

"Are you sure we shouldn't just write a letter?" She asked as they went out the students' building and headed down the graveled path towards the teachers' offices.

"No, we will do asking," Jimmy said.

"Yes, we should!" Zack added. "We are adults and adults have door keys. I know. My mum is an adult, she has one. My dad is an adult, he has one. My aunt is an adult and she has one. For *her* house. My granddad is an adult…"

"Okay Zack, we get it!" Polly snapped.

"I would like to hear it," Jimmy said.

"Okay. My Granddad is an adult and he has one. My neighbor, Dray, he is an adult and he has one. His son is seven months old so he does not have a key. But he does have some plastic keys that are a toy but do not open the front door. My sister is an adult and she has one. My cousin..."

Polly groaned. She prided herself on being a patient person and normally she could keep her cool. But normally she didn't have the likes of Jimmy Tiffin stirring things up and asking so many questions. And what was with the camera he carried with him everywhere? It made things all the more difficult, knowing every second of your life was being documented.

"Jimmy, will you put that camera down?" She asked as they got to the entrance of the teachers offices.

"No. I want to do filming and I am an adult so why can I not?"

"Because not everyone wants to be watched all the time!"

"But we are watched all the time. We have staff and workers and we do not even have keys so we can lock our door," Jimmy said.

"Oh for God's sake, fine then," Polly conceded as she punched in the code to the teachers' building.

Outside the principal's office Polly knocked on the door and stepped back behind the three lads.

"Come in!" A deep voice called from inside.

"Okay!" Jimmy called back and opened the door.

"So how can I help you gents?" The heavy set principle, George, asked them once all three were settled on hard backed chairs in front of him, Jimmy with his camera on his lap pointed at George, Polly hovering nervously in the corner.

"We are adults," Jimmy said. "And we would like to have a door key."

"Ah," said George looking over to Polly. "The thing is that there are rules, as you *should* have been told. And one of these rules is that you can not have your own door key."

"I told them that Mr Jacobs, but they wanted to come here anyway."

"Okay then boys, so why is it you want a key."

"Because… my Cousin is an adult and he has one. And My Sister is fourteen and she has one. And my uncle is an adult and he has one…" Zack said.

"I think he gets it," Polly snapped.

"Adults have door keys," Jimmy said, ignoring Polly.

"It is so the room is yours," Robert said, "and things can be private."

"Okay," said George, appearing to mull this over. "But what if you lose it? And then someone else finds it and gets into your room and steals all your things?"

"Um… I don't know," Zack said looking at Jimmy.

"Do you have a door key?" Jimmy asked George,

"Yes."

"But what if you do losing and someone steals your things."

"Then it is my fault and I replace them."

"Then why isn't it our fault?"

"Okay…" Said George, needing to think now. "What if someone gets stuck in their room?"

"What if you got stuck in your room?"

"It's different for me."

"Why?"

"Because you... you have special needs?"

"But why does that mean I will lose a key or get stuck? I have not been stuck before and I have lost a jumper once but my dad has a key and he lost a jacket and a bag and one time he lost his car but then found it again. Why can't we have a key?"

"Because... because... can you turn that camera off now Jimmy?"

"No, I would like to keep it on. I told Mary and Helen and Tony and Rachel and Paul and Scott and they said they would like keys but Polly said she wouldn't take them here so I said I would film it and show them as so they can see it as well."

"There are more of you who want keys?"

"Yes!" Robert said. "We would like to have room keys!"

George looked at each one of them, then at Polly, then at the camera and he ended up resting his eyes angrily on Polly.

"I'll see what I can do," he said.

Three days later and Jimmy, Robert and Zack sat together in the lounge, holding their keys. They had ones for their rooms, not the front door to the accommodation which was locked at night, nor for the lounge or the kitchen cupboards. But at least they'd made a start. And more than that, other people in other rooms had been given keys too. They'd made a real difference and each of them could feel it. The first fight they'd won and it felt good. For Jimmy it felt like they were still losing around seven hundred and sixty eight to one, but at least he had that one now. At least he was on the scoreboard.

10

"Here you go," Lilly said, handing Sally a knee length, tight black skirt.

"Okay," Sally said taking it from her friend. "Thank you."

"You look very beautiful!" Lilly said when Sally had put the skirt on with her strapped purple top.

"Thank you. You too," Sally said, looking at herself in the mirror and allowing herself a smile.

"Okay, we have got to wear this perfume," Lilly said, taking an opaque, crystal shaped bottle down from the shelf that ran above her bed. "It is the one with the advert that is black and white and it is very good."

She sprayed some on herself first, then gave Sally's neck and shoulders a light dusting before carefully putting it back on the shelf.

When they were ready Lilly's mum drove them to the address they had been given. It was supported living accommodation in the next town over, enough room for four young people. There were two girls and two guys living there, Paul introduced them to Dianna and Hannah who he and Sammy lived with and their support workers Rich, Dev and Debra.

"Rich lives here actually," Paul said as Lilly, Sally and Teresa shook hands with their new acquaintances. "Debra and Dev are supporting us with going out tonight. We have to be back by ten O'clock as that's when they go home. We are getting two taxis there and back."

"That's good," Teresa said. "Well, I'll get out of your hair then guys and girls. See you later girls, be safe. Call me when you want picking up," She added, kissing Lilly and Sally on the cheeks and heading out.

"Mum just wanted to meet you," Lilly told them.

"Okay," Paul said smiling at her. "That's good. She is nice actually."

"She is. Why do we go back by ten? On Eastenders they party all night and we are the same age as them as they are also nineteen?"

"Yeah, but our shifts finish at ten," Dev said with an inhalation of breath to suggest he was already going above and beyond the call of duty.

"What time are we going?" Sally asked the group.

"Soon as we are ready," Hannah said.

"Okay. Are you looking forward to going out?"

"Yes," Hannah and Dianna said.

"How about you Sammy?"

"Yes," Sammy nodded opening up the book in front of him. "I am feeling this," he said handing her a picture card that had the word 'excited' written upon it with a picture of a smiling stick man. "I have these to say what I'm feeling."

"Good," Lilly said. "I have seen them at school and at college as some people use them sometimes, why do you not use them in college?"

"I only use them sometimes like when I am nervous or excited."

"Or both," Dev said, giving him a playful nudge in the ribs with his elbow. "Come on then, let's get our things together and mosey."

Once everyone had got their coats and shoes on, Rich called up a taxi company and the group went outside and waited in the cold. Sammy, Lilly and Hannah all lit up cigarettes. From what Sally could tell Paul and Hannah were something of an item, they kept holding hands and sharing quick smiles. Sally liked them all; they all seemed friendly and eager to make her feel welcome.

"Do you have support workers?" Hannah asked her.

"No. I would like some though so I can do clubbing more often but I sometimes need help with some things."

"You should talk to services as they can give you support workers."

"Okay."

"If you'd like some help, come into our offices one day. I'll give you the address later on if you'd like," Rich said to her.

"Okay," Sally said nodding.

The taxis came and they all piled in. Sally was nervous; she'd never done anything like this before. She watched out the window, looking at all the other teenagers wandering about, heading into pubs all in their groups.

I've got a group now, she thought to herself, looking around the taxi at her friends. She'd always wanted a group like this but figured it wasn't going to happen. When she used to live with her mum at their old place she'd sometimes watch out the upstairs window on a Friday or Saturday night and wish she could be out there like all the other young people, hanging out, drinking and smoking. Now she could. She'd have a cigarette later, she decided. Just because she could.

They got into town about fifteen minutes later. The taxi dropped them off on the high street and Paul paid the driver with just a bit of help from Rich. Sally had some money tonight that she'd taken from her stockpile under the bed. Every time she was given some money, she saved the change just in case. She'd taken all five of the notes and a pocket full of change as she wasn't sure how much things were going to be costing.

They met up with the others and wandered down the high street then out a bit the other side. Sally wasn't too sure what they meant by clubbing but when she saw the large football clubhouse with flashing lights around the edge and music hammering out, she felt her excitement peak. It dropped slightly when she went inside however; to see that all the people inside were people with disabilities.

But even so, it was buzzing. The bar was packed with smartly dressed men and women queuing for drinks, the dance floor was already being used by at least twenty five people, there were balloons, flashing lights and a DJ booth in the corner with a man spinning songs, some that Sally recognized from the radio. There were support workers, but most were making themselves scarce around the edges, sipping cokes and chatting quietly in little groups as if they too were there for a party.

"Let's get a drink!" Sammy said, taking Lilly's arm awkwardly and leading the group over to join the crowd at the bar.

When they had paid for their drinks, they headed outside for another cigarette. Outside people were laughing and jostling, drinking and smoking. People smiled at her as they walked past and you could still hear the music through the doors.

They finished their drinks outside and went and bought another. One more and Sammy worked up the courage to ask Lilly if she'd like to dance.

Lilly blushed and looked to the floor, speechless for the first time before nodding and holding out her hand, curtseying a little. He smiled and bowed, took her hand and they went and stood opposite each other, smiling and dancing, trying not to catch each others eyes. Paul and Hannah were already dancing in each others arms.

"You enjoying yourself?" Dianna asked.

"Yes thank you. Are you?" Sally replied.

"Yes. I like the music here, they play all the rap songs that are very cool. Do you like rap music?"

"Yes, Rap music is very good. I like rap music."

"Me to. It is good with the rapping."

The girls lapsed into silence as they leant back against the wall and watched the dancers go for it.

There was someone who caught Sally's eye. A young man wearing a checkered shirt was dancing in the corner with his friends. He wasn't going over the top, like his friend who was trying to dance with every girl who went past, kissing hands and grabbing waists. But the guy in the checkered shirt, he didn't need to, he was just standing, dancing, looking pretty cool. She wasn't even the only one to notice, there were two other girls dancing near him, hoping that he'd dance with them.

It wasn't like her to be like this, she met a lot of guys, but there was something about him that also seemed so approachable, like she'd met him before. So she wandered over to where he was dancing, with Dianna close behind her, and she started to dance almost next to him, glancing over to the man whose face she could barely see under his long hair. She noticed him glance once or twice towards her too and she hoped he'd noticed her. That was when she realized she'd seen him before, around her college, he was the one who looked a little like Jimmy and that was why she was drawn to him. But thinking of Jimmy made her step back a pace or two from this guy. What was wrong with her, she wondered. Why could she not get over Jimmy?

After half an hour or so of dancing, Dianna asked her if she wanted a cigarette. She didn't want to leave the building, but she didn't want to dance alone so she agreed and they went outside the centre and stood by the doorway, next to other groups or pairs who were standing and smoking.

Dianna lit one up and passed one to Sally, who lit the second cigarette of her life. It didn't taste nice and straight away she started coughing.

"Did you see the man near us?" Sally asked when she had recovered.

"With long hair like a girl?" Diana asked, with no hint of mockery.

"Yes."

"Yes."

"He is nice."

"I liked the man who was doing all the dancing," said Dianna, thinking of the friend. "He was very good."

They were just about to go in when Sally felt a tap on her shoulder. She turned around and her heart leapt to see the man with the long hair standing behind her.

"Hello," he said. "I have seen you here and at coffee house and at my college when I have gone for link," he said. "You are very pretty," he added quickly turning a deep shade of red under his hair.

"Thank you," Sally said. "I have seen you too. You are very good at dancing."

"Would you like to dance with me?" He asked.

"Yes," Sally said, looking to the floor. "Yes I would like that please."

He took her hand, stirring up dormant feelings in her chest and let him lead her inside. She was glad he was doing this, but still she couldn't help feeling like she did all that time ago when Charlie had tried to kiss her, when her and Jimmy were still an item.

Although the song was an up tempo indie track, he put his hands on her shoulders, as she did him and they danced slowly. They both kept eyes on their feet and rocked backwards and forwards, getting closer and closer. She could feel him look-ing at her and she let him, her breaths were getting deeper and heavier, but… but there was that something, just a… a something that was wrong.

He leant up and kissed her cheek and then she leant back and they let their lips meet and then she knew what was wrong. She didn't want to feel like this for anyone other then Jimmy.

She quickly stepped back.

"Sorry," she said, "but I am in love with only Jimmy Tiffin!"

Then she turned from the dance floor and walked quickly out the building, leaving the young man confused and alone.

Outside she stopped to catch her breath, leaning against a concrete pillar, with her eyes closed and wondering if she could ever really be happy without him, without her Jimmy.

She let herself slide down the pillar and sat, arms across her knees, head on her arms like she hadn't sat in some time.

A few minutes later and she felt a tap on her arms.

"But I am confused," said the young man she'd been dancing with, brushing his hair back behind his ears.

"Why?" Sally asked.

"Because I am Jimmy Tiffin."

Suddenly it clicked for both of them; both stared at each other, mouths open.

"Jimmy!" Sally shouted jumping up. "But you are at college far away!"

"It is not far away. It is in this town," said Jimmy, "I thought you were far away!"

"No, I am in this town. At college!"

"I…I…I…" Jimmy tried.

"I am so happy!" Sally shouted, and threw her arms around him. This time when their lips met there was nothing that felt wrong, everything was perfect. They kissed quickly, repeatedly and then both started laughing, Jimmy eyes were watering, everything was so perfect.

Then, when they were ready, they walked back in together. Together again. Neither feeling like they'd ever been apart.

Which in a very real way, they hadn't.

II

Jimmy was sat in his common room with Robert, Zack and a few others from the dorm. It was the day of the end of term and they'd been packing their things up ready for their parents to come and pick them up in a few hours time.

Generally it had been a good year. The work had been much like it had been at Hollygroves' post sixteen, which had been a bit frustrating, but they'd enjoyed learning about shopping, travelling and budgeting. And best of all of course for Jimmy, he had found Sally again.

Jimmy parents, along with Tim, were as always the first to arrive. Jimmy's mum swept him up into her arms and hugged him so tightly it began to hurt.

"How you doing Jim?" Tim asked, smiling and holding out his hand for Jimmy to shake, which he did.

"I am okay thank you Tim and how are you?" Jimmy asked.

"I'm good thanks," Tim said smiling.

"Right, should we get the car loaded up?" His dad asked.

"Yes and I will help!" Robert said.

"Yes and I will help as well if you would like me to," Zack said jumping up alongside his friends.

In the car on the way back, they were all quiet. Jimmy was thinking about the long summer away from Sally, who was of course staying up with her mum. But it would be nice to see his old town and his old friends, hopefully go on some of the adult activity groups. And then, back to College in September for another two years. And then? And then, who knew. He had some meetings at college coming up with some teachers to help him think about that. Jimmy didn't mind the un-known too much, as long as he got to do it with his friends and his Sally. They were all in this together now. And it felt good.

Adulthood

I

Jimmy could barely sit still during the car journey. The whole way his knee bounced up and down underneath the same suitcase that he had, had on his lap those three years ago when he was on his way to college. Once again his mum and dad were driving him but this time Tim was sitting on his right and Sam was on the other side. The car was full with accumulated belongs, so much so that the people carrier his Dad still drove was packed to the brim.

This time they weren't going to any education institution. This time he was going home. To his new home. Jimmy was more excited than he'd ever been before; this was the start of his new life, where he would get a job and live as an adult. This was his beginning. Another beginning.

And more than that, he thought as they pulled up outside his new home, he was getting to live with Sally. It would be him, Robert, Sally and Lilly living with a support worker. It was going to be great! He had seen his old acquaintance Charlie a little while ago on one of the adult activity groups, and Charlie was going to stay living with his parents, they couldn't find anything for him. But Jimmy and his gang were going to have their own space, their own home, their own castle, thanks to the work of the local adult services team and Lilly's mum who had worked out the logistics and applied for the house.

Jimmy's mum wasn't all that happy. For a start, the house was further away then she'd liked. And on top of that he was living with the girl who had been nothing but trouble for him. That's how she saw it anyhow. This girl who he never stopped talking to or about. Maybe she was jealous, Mrs Tiffin conceded. It wouldn't be un-reasonable; after all she felt like she'd had to do almost everything for him for so long, maybe she had assumed he'd always need her in that way and now this girl…

But this was the way things were. In the eyes of the law and the services, he was an adult. And adults got to choose where they lived and what they did. And this is what he had chosen.

The new home was a modern, terraced house on the edge of the town in which they grew up. It was part of a smart development where every house looked the same and every street was named after a species of bird. Number 7 Falcon road was their new home.

Inside the house was a decent size, two double rooms, two singles and a box room/study with about enough room for a single bed and possibly a desk. They had already decided that the girls would have the doubles, the men the singles and the live in support worker would get the box room.

All four of the others were already there and came to the door to greet him.

"Jimmy!" Sally shouted as he struggled up the driveway and came to give him a hug which he tried to return, burdened as he was with bags.

"Sally. How are you?"

"Fine thank you."

"Good," Jimmy said enjoying the moment.

"Hello Sally," his mum said, stepping in and taking her hand from her son's waist so she could shake it as the others stepped up as well.

"My name is Lilly and I am going to help with the bags because I know where things should go," Lilly told his mum who pulled as much of a smile towards the young girl as she could manage.

"Okay then," she said.

"And I can carry loads of things because I have a gym membership and I'm going to be a wrestler," said Robert, flexing his muscles underneath his tight, white t-shirt.

"Hi guys," said the adult, around thirty, who'd been hanging back, "I'm Duncan, the live in support worker. Nice to see you again Jimmy." He extended his hand and took Jimmy's firmly in his own, before taking his mums that had been hovering. "Let me take those," he added, motioning towards the bags Mrs Tiffin had momentarily put down.

Once Jimmy's stuff was in his room and his family had said the tearful goodbyes, they all met together in the kitchen sitting around the dining table.

"Right guys, how we liking the place?" Duncan asked them.

"Good," Sally said.

"I like my room and the lounge with the big television where we can watch films," Jimmy said.

"Good. Well I just wanted to suggest a few things that I think would be good. Firstly, the day after tomorrow, I'd like to take you into the local adult services centre where you can meet lots of people like job advisors and youth group leaders."

"Will the job centre be where I get my job working with films?" Jimmy asked.

"They can certainly try mate," Duncan said nodding. "They'll help you however they can."

"Okay."

"The other thing guys, is how you'd like to use your house. The only things that are certain are because the council funds this place; we have to stick to some rules. We can't smoke inside and we can't wreck the place. We have to keep it tidy. How do you think the best way to do that is?"

"Rota?" Asked Robert, who'd learnt about them in his life skills classes.

"Great idea Robert. You guys agree?"

They all nodded.

"Great. We can do that in a bit. Before that I'd like to tell you more about what I do. I sleep here every night through the week, and I help in the mornings and evenings. I work at a drugs rehab centre through the day, so you'll have to stay safe and do your own things. You can find out about a lot of things to do at the information fayre at the adult services centre, there's a lot to do if you'd like. I have weekends off where I'll be sleeping here most nights, but someone else will be in if you want support. If you get angry with me or you'd like to complain, you can call the number that is in the tray by the toaster. Any questions so far?"

They all shook their heads. This had been explained when they were setting it all up.

"Great. Ask if you need anything. While I'm around, I'm here to help."

"Do you do cooking?" Sally asked. "I'd like to do cooking."

"We'll split all the housework five ways. That includes cooking. But if you want to do extra cooking, then maybe when it's my turn to do the cooking, then I can do your job and you can do mine. We can swap. Is that okay?"

"That is okay. I am good at cooking."

"That's cool, I'm terrible!" Duncan said chuckling. "Right, I hope you don't mind but I've made up some packs for you. They've got phone numbers and information and my 'about me' guide." He produced some laminated folders from a plastic bag which had been by his side. On the front was a picture of the house. Jimmy took his and started reading through. Each page was made up of pictures and words in large font, which helped him understand it better then he thought he was going to. There were sections on his money which came from his benefits, around living, the rules, who to call in an emergency. The whole thing held a lot of information, but was also pocket sized somehow. He made a mental note to always carry it with him. His excitement was beginning to become nerves; it seemed being an adult wasn't just having a key and looking for a job.

"Shall we do a Rota now?" Sally asked.

"Yeah!" Robert said.

"Great. I thought you might like to do one, so I've already started," Duncan said. "I made you a grid with your names on it and took some photos of rooms and things we'd need to do. Enough for the week. All we gotta do is decide which photo goes where at what time. Or you can make your own?"

"We'll use this one. It is nice," Sally said.

"I can draw some pictures to make it more colorful because I like drawing pictures like suns and flowers and moons and people?" Lilly asked.

"Sounds great," Duncan said, "let's make a start, shall we?"

When the Rota was done, they pinned it up to the wall in the kitchen. All of them stood back and looked at it together. Sally slipped a hand into Jimmy's and both felt electric as their palms met and fingers interlocked. They had put photos up next to their names in the left hand column and Lilly had decorated it with flowers, birds and trees. All four stared in silence for eight minutes as the enormity of the day dawned on them. This was their home. They would miss their friends from college, but they were home now. This was their life. This was their beginning.

2

Sally woke up for the second night running, pushing herself into the wall on the edge of her double bed. It felt big, too big; she wondered fleetingly if she'd ever share it with Jimmy, like couples did in her soap operas and her sitcoms. She guessed that one day they might, they were sort of an item now, she wouldn't dream of kissing anyone else, but they hadn't had that conversation and she was beginning to worry if they ever would.

She rolled over and looked at her digital clock which red digits told her it was nine O'clock. They were going to the information event in three hours, so she could have had another hour of sleep, but she decided instead to get up and go and make her breakfast.

Their food was bought using their benefits which they had decided to pool together. Duncan had taught them about budgeting and how much money they had left after the money had gone out for the house and they had decided that sixty three pounds a week should pay for enough food for the four of them since Duncan got his own. They had been shopping the day before, so the cupboards were pretty well stocked.

Sally made herself a bowl of cereal and took this into the lounge where Lilly was sitting and watching morning cartoons.

"Good morning Sally, I slept well and I hope you slept well," Lilly said to her.

"Hi," Sally replied, settling down next to her friend, comfortable to watch the program aimed for younger people because Lilly was too.

Once they were all up, dressed and ready to go, Duncan drove them down into town to the community hall which was being used for the fayre. They all went in together and when they got inside they were struck by the sheer amount of stalls, things to look at and people to talk to.

"Hey, Dave, Julie!" Duncan called to a middle-aged man in a wheelchair being pushed around by an older lady. "Let me introduce you to the crew I'm living with."

"Hi," the group responded waving. Dave looked up and managed a smile, before lifting his hand up and letting it drop by his side.

"How'd you do?" Julie asked the group politely.

"We are good as we are here for the information about being an adult," Lilly told her.

"Sounds good," Julie said smiling at them. "Well, we're just off to grab a coffee so we'll see you around the fayre."

"Okay, we'll see you around the fayre," Lilly said.

"Right, where'd you guys want to go?" Duncan asked them after Julie and Dave had moved on.

"Where do I go to work in films?" Jimmy asked.

"Or be a wrestler?" Robert asked.

"Okay, let's start with making you each a home appointment with 'Work Now.' They are a company that helps people get jobs. Then we can go from there."

The five of them made a beeline to the far end of hall where the 'Work Now' desk was situated. The had to wait a minute or two while a young man in front of them made an appointment, then they signed themselves up for a meeting in two days time with the smiling lady behind the desk. She wrote their names down in the diary and then gave them a few sweets and a pen with the 'Work Now,' website address printed along the side. When they'd done this they started making their way clockwise around the room, picking up information, chatting to the people running the stalls and gathering more sweets, pens and stickers.

About a third of the way round Duncan put his hand on Jimmy's shoulder and bent down to his ear.

"Come with me a minute mate, got someone I want you to meet," he said quietly. Ahead of them the others were talking to representatives of a football club for young men and women with disabilities, so Jimmy let himself be led back the way they came.

"Now, you and Sally, are you in a relationship?" Duncan asked once they were out of the other's earshot.

"Yes," Jimmy answered.

"And have you had sex?"

Jimmy didn't answer, but managed to blush crimson and shake his head just a little.

"Okay. Well, what I think we should do is go and get some information about it all, just in case. Would you like to have children soon?"

"No. Not yet."

"That's very sensible mate. Okay. Then we should get information on how to stay safe. There's no pressure to do anything, but in case you do, best be prepared. You understand? I'll do this with everyone else we live with as well, but since we're here and you and Sally are so close…"

"Okay," Jimmy said, looking at the floor.

"Okay then," said Duncan, patting his back supportively.

The sex and relationships stall was at the opposite end to where they'd started. Jimmy looked around as they approached it, feeling embarrassed but unsure as to why. In nearly every film he'd watched there was sex somewhere in there, it was never presented as a bad or wrong thing. But still he felt anxious as he looked up to see an extremely pretty brunette lady sitting behind the stall.

"Hi," the lady said once they were in front of her. "How can I help?"

"Hi," Duncan said returning her smile.

Jimmy kept his eyes down on his tapping foot.

"We're looking for some information about sex," Duncan said, having given Jimmy a couple of moments to respond but realizing he wasn't going to.

"Okay. Well, we have plenty of information here. We have leaflets, videos and books. Most of the important bits you can find in our information pack, however. Would you like to take a pack young man?" she asked Jimmy, holding out a yellow folder.

"Okay," said Jimmy, taking it from her without meeting her eyes and putting it straight into his rucksack.

"Now, there's plenty in there to read in your own time and also numbers to call should you need any further information and condoms for just in case or if you want some practice. It's probably not the best place to talk here, about your personal plans, so maybe you could take this away and have a think. Then if you'd like to know more you can call us up, make an appointment or visit the website."

"Okay," Jimmy replied nodding quickly, looking forward to moving on from this stall.

"Okay," the lady said smiling at both of them.

"Thanks," Duncan said, smiling back and putting his hand on Jimmy shoulder so he could guide the young man back to his friends.

They caught up with the rest of their group at the bar which was at the back of the hall and was serving hot drinks and snacks. Robert, Lilly and Sally had got themselves coffees and were talking to some people about the community centre they were in.

"Is it good here when you do activities on a Friday night rather then when you have an information fair with lots of people and information?" Lilly asked.

"Yes, yes, yes very good here," a young man wearing a denim jacket was saying, gesticulating exaggeratedly as he did.

"What do you do?"

"Very good. Good time here. You come here? Very good."

"Okay."

"Yes, okay. Very good here, good fun here. You come here?"

"No. But we might do if it's rocking!" Robert said.

"Okay. Very good. Very good here."

"Okay," Sally said, "maybe we will come here and do activities."

"Glad to here it," said a man, about fifty, from over the young man's shoulders. "Have you got our timetable?"

"Yes we have got your timetable as this is a fayre and we got a lot of leaflets and one of them was your timetable," Lilly said.

"Excellent, I'll hope to see you about then."

"Yes," Lilly said. "We are adults and adults go to clubs."

Back at their home, two hours later, Robert, Lilly and Sally laid out their information in the lounge while Jimmy took his up to his room. Once there he sat on his bed and looked inside the folder that the lady had given him. It was filled with information about reproduction and sexually transmitted diseases, set out so he could easily understand, with pictures, big font and not too many words. He had learnt some of this in school, but had never seen condoms in anything other than pictures before. He wondered briefly if he and Sally would ever have sex or not. He wanted to; he thought about it most days, but he was nervous, didn't know what to expect, wanted to make sure she enjoyed it but wasn't sure. It was in all his films, sex was everywhere he looked and like all men his age, he felt that urge to do it, that tingle when he saw it happening on the screen. But he was nervous.

At the back of the folder he found the condoms the lady had said were there. There were five of them altogether, along with information on how to put them on. The information was set out in pictures, like the rest, and one of the pictures showed how you could practice putting them on. He opened one of them up and had a look; it felt different to how he thought it was going to and he didn't think it would be so stretchy.

Just then, he heard his name being called from downstairs by Robert so he quickly put the folder away in the bottom of his wardrobe and draped a coat over the top, threw the condom in the bin, then he went to find his friends to start pawing through the other bits of information that they had collected.

3

Robert walked past Jimmy using long, purposeful strides, eyes down. Jimmy wanted to say something, but didn't know what. And anyway, it was his turn to speak to the careers lady, so he got up from the sofa and went through to the kitchen.

At the table Duncan and the careers officers were having a hushed, heated conversation. Jimmy only caught a couple of words before they saw him and stopped abruptly. Those words were 'realistic goals.' He wasn't sure what that meant, so he sat down un-perturbed.

"Hi Jimmy, my names Sheila," the lady said from behind thick rimmed glasses, "I see you want to work in films?" She added, looking down at his 'personal planning' folder which he'd completed in school and had been up-dating since.

"Yes. I want to do films."

"Okay. And have you had any work experience working with films?"

"I have a film camera and have sixty nine hours and thirty two minutes and nine seconds of film that I have put on my computer."

"Okay. And what kind of films do you like?" She asked, sighing so softly it could have been a breath.

"I like films like a film about a man in a mask who sets off fireworks and saves a girl. But I don't like it when the detective hands a rose to someone as one minute it is covered in plastic and the next minute it is not and then it is again."

"Oh. Okay. Well, it's very hard to get a job working with films. We have to look at what's realistic. How about we look for jobs like working in a video shop? Or working in a café? It says here you're very good at making cups of tea and sandwiches?"

"I thought you would get me a job in films?" Jimmy asked, deflating a bit, but so used to conversations like this now. If she wouldn't help him, he'd just keep looking until someone did.

"Well, like I said, jobs like that are very hard to get into. But would you like a different job while you try, *in your own time*, to work in films?"

Jimmy thought for a moment.

"Yes. Many people who work in films have other jobs first. I would like a job so I can have money so that I can do shopping and buy films."

"Okay. Well what we need to do in that case is update the CV you have in your folder, then I can give you an idea of where to look and you could go out and try to get a job. I can also take your number and call you if I hear about a job I think you might like. Sound good?"

"Okay."

"Right then, shall we start?"

It took them ten minutes to update the CV then a further fifteen minutes typing it up on Duncan's laptop. When it was done, they printed it off twenty five times and Duncan gave the pile to Jimmy with a supportive smile, laced with undertones of apology that Jimmy didn't notice.

"That okay mate?" He asked him.

"Okay," Jimmy said. "I will look for another job until I can do filming."

"Sounds good. Maybe you could write a letter to a film studio, see if they can take you on as work experience?"

"Okay!" Said Jimmy, brightening instantly. "Will you help with spelling and sentences?"

"Sure can mate."

"Okay," said Jimmy, before walking back to his room with decidedly more flourish then Robert had done.

When he passed Sally, who was waiting where he had, he smiled at her.

"Your turn," he said.

"Okay, good," Sally said and got up off the sofa.

When she got into the kitchen the hushed conversation was slightly more animated this time, again stopping when she came in, their frowns turning to synchronized smiles.

"So Sally," Shelia said as Sally sat down. "It says here you'd like to be chef?"

"I am very good at cooking," Sally said to her.

"Okay. Maybe we could look at getting you work in a café or a restaurant helping out?"

"Okay," said Sally.

"Let's have a look, shall we?"

Sally didn't know why she stopped when she had left the kitchen and closed the door. She didn't know why she decided to listen in. Maybe it was their faces when she first went it, maybe it was their hushed conversation. But she did stop and she found if she got really close and put her ear to the door, she could hear them talking:

"Well I'm sorry if I have to be realistic," Shelia was saying.

"Couldn't you have at least listened to their dreams?" Duncan said, his tone with an edge Sally hadn't heard before.

"A wrestler? A chef? An office boss and a film director? I'm sorry Duncan, but few able people get these jobs, let alone *disa*bled people. They should be lucky to have a job at all, let alone these fantasies. They have disabilities, you need to accept that."

"They have dreams. You need to accept that."

"I do. But when I was younger I had a dream of being a famous singer. I let it go when I realized I can't sing. Get the point?"

"How can you dismiss them like this?"

"Because I've seen it happen a hundred times before. *You* raise their dreams, *you* watch the dreams get dashed and *you* pick up the pieces. I'm going to try and help them earn some money and gain some self respect."

"I'm not giving up," Duncan said sighing.

"You will do soon," Shelia said, her voice softening. "You will."

4

All five of them ate dinner together in relative silence. Sally had cooked an impressive risotto, which they all tucked into, but she hadn't made it with her usual heart. Even though it had been three days ago, she still couldn't get the conversation out of her head, couldn't understand why that woman wouldn't listen to what they wanted and help them out. There were many chefs and wrestlers, bosses and directors out there, why couldn't they do that? She knew they weren't like other people, had been reminded and reminded of this all her life, but that shouldn't stop them; should it? Sally knew she could cook, Jimmy knew more about films then anyone she'd ever met, probably anyone ever. That was all it took. Right?

"You guys looking forward to the club tonight?" Duncan ventured, trying to liven the spirits of all but Jimmy who was the only one in a positive frame of mind.

"Yes," Jimmy said.

"Did you send those letters in the end Jimmy?" Duncan said.

"Yes. I put it in the post this morning when I went to get paper and milk."

"Good, good," Duncan said, enjoying the lad's optimism.

The day before they had written a letter about Jimmy and his interests included his CV, printed four out, put them in envelopes and addressed them to four film companies in London. Jimmy was particularly interested in one up and coming company, 'Showdown pictures,' who'd recently released a few films that he'd really liked. Now all that was left was a waiting game.

"When will they help me get a job?" Jimmy asked.

"We'll have to wait and see mate," Duncan told him, "we'll have to wait and see. And for the mean time, you guys are all going to town tomorrow to see what you can find, right?"

"Yes, we will go do job hunting in town," said Lilly.

"Good. Everyone starts off small guys, let's get you jobs then see where it goes from there."

"Okay, we will do starting off small."

Once Jimmy and Robert had washed and dried up they went to their separate rooms to get ready then, once dressed, they congregated in the lounge. Sally was pleased to see Robert was wearing a shirt and Lilly had put on that red skirt she looked so pretty in. Both seemed in better spirits when they were dressed up.

"Hi Sally. Are you ready to go to activity?" Lilly asked.

"Yes," said Sally, who had thrown on her favorite pink t-shirt and a pair of jeans.

"Good," Lilly replied, smiling properly for the first time in a couple of days.

The five of them went and got in Duncan's reasonably new, silver Renault and they set off down to the club.

At the gates Duncan dropped them off.

"Call me if ya need anything," he said before shooting off to the nearest pub to watch a football match with his friends.

"Can I have a cigarette before we go in?" Lilly asked them as they stood outside the same community centre the information fayre had been in.

"Yes," said Robert, "and can I borrow one please? It's been a loooonng day!"

"Okay," Lilly said and handed him one over with her lighter.

Once the cigarettes had been smoked and Robert had stopped coughing they went in. Inside was different to last time at the fayre; the bar was serving all kinds of drinks, not just tea and coffee, there were less people and it seemed so much bigger without all the stalls. The room was pretty full of people aged between nineteen and seventy five either milling around and chatting or sitting on chairs around the edge.

"Hi, you must be our new recruits. I'm Sophie," a middle aged lady in a flowery dress said to them after noticing them come in. "You've joined us at the best time."

"What activity are we doing today?" Lilly asked her. "We have the time table but on the time table it just said a meeting and the same for the next week and week after that unlike the other days, before today, which said cocktail making or bowling or going out to eat."

"That's right, we're going to have a meeting to decide what event to put on over Christmas this year. Every year we do something. Last year we put on a play for people to come and watch and the year before that was a winter sports day. Help yourselves to tea, coffee or something from the bar. We're going to start in about fifteen minutes."

"Okay," Sally said. She used to be nervous in these types of situations and she still felt the odd flutter. She only had to look at her group though and most of the butterflies seemed to fly away.

They went and got themselves two bottles of lager and two ciders from the bar, each paying in turn with the ten pounds that they had come out with that evening. By the time they'd done this and turned around, a circle of hard backed chairs interspersed with spaces for people in wheelchairs had appeared and people were beginning to move and fill them.

Jimmy, Robert, Sally and Lilly took four seats near some people who seemed to be more their age. The people around the circle had seemed to naturally do this, migrate into age ranges in groups of five or six. Next to Lilly sat a lad of about twenty five she guessed, but then she was never very good at guessing.

"Helloooo," he said to her. "You alright mate?"

"I'm okay thank you. My name is Lilly and it is my first time here and it is nice."

"Oh! That's good then!" The young man exclaimed with a large smile.

"Good," Lilly said, smiling now. *He's handsome,* she thought, with his dark skin and round face. He was wearing a purple shirt and suit trousers over formal shoes and a thin gold chain around his neck.

"I like your skirt. It's red like Man United!" He said to her.

"Thank you. It is a skirt I bought with my money while doing shopping in town centre shops like New Look."

"That's good then! Do they have lots of red clothes in there?"

"Yes they have some red clothes and some other colors to."

"Excellent! That rocks!"

"Does it?"

"Yes!"

"Good," said Lilly, smiling wider even then before.

"Okay then guys!" Said Sophie, standing up in the middle of the thirty odd chairs and smiling at the assembled group. "Today we're going to talk about our Christmas event. As you can see there are a few new faces around, I hope you have a chance to meet them this evening. And for those of you who don't know, we hold a Christmas event every year. We've done plays; we've done Casino evenings, fetes... too many to count! Now we have a few suggestions that our panel have decided on and the first thing we need to do is vote. Okay, what we got Dan?"

She turned to a thirty something man holding a piece of paper, who sat next to the chair she'd vacated to speak and that she took up once again.

"We narrowed down to there..." Dan started reading.

"Three," Sophie interjected

"Three ideas," Dan continued in a mumbling voice, before handing the piece of paper he was reading from to a woman on his left.

"The ideas are…" The woman said, standing briefly before handing the paper to a man in a wheelchair on her left. He smiled and took the piece of paper awkwardly, only able to hold it between his thumb and little finger. He put the piece of paper down on the tray attached to his wheelchair and started reading, unable to articulate at all, but giving it his best shot, making non-distinct sounds that were as close to words as he could manage.

Sophie waited until he was finished then interpreted for him.

"Charity bake sale and auction," she said.

The man then passed the paper to his left, to an older man of around sixty who theatrically put his glasses on.

"Or we could do a carol singing day with some mulled wine and some CAKE!" He said, punching the air at the last word, evoking cheers from the audience around him.

"I like cake!" Shouted a woman to the left of Jimmy's group.

"Me too!" Said the man who had spoken, then he passed the paper to a woman who stood slowly with the aid of a stick. She held the paper at her side, clearly having memorized her line so she could stand.

"Or – we – could – do – a – par – ty – with – drinks – and – D – J – and – other – stuff – like – dancing – and – 'tertainment," she said, before slowly sitting down.

"Okay!" Sophie said, standing up again. "I'm going to pass around some paper and pens. Please write which idea you like best on the paper. So, if you'd like the bake sale and auction, write number one. If you'd like the carol singing, write number two. And if you'd like a party, write number three. Rob, Hope and Fred over there by the bar are here to help if you need any.

Then when you're done, fold the paper up and come give it to me so we can get counting!"

Once the gang had written their choices on the paper they went and handed them to Sophie who put them all in an empty bucket. Then they went back up to the bar to grab another drink.

"Hi again!" The man who had sat next to Lilly said to her as they wandered outside so she could smoke. He was there with another couple of lads all of whom had lit cigarettes in their hands.

"Hi," Lilly said, "I'm Lilly and these are my best friends and my house mates, Sally, Robert and Jimmy. What are your names?"

"Excellent!" said the man. "My name is Kyle and these are my friends Jason and Gregory!"

"Hi," Jason said giving a four fingered wave.

Gregory waved and beamed a large smile.

"What did you choose for the paper?" Lilly asked Kyle.

"I love parties. Do you love parties?" He replied.

"Yes. I also chose party. As did my friends. We like parties."

"Well that's good!" He said. "Excellent!"

Sally and Jimmy were standing together watching the others smoke when suddenly Jimmy got a tap on his shoulder from behind.

"Hullo Jimmy!" Aalap called. "Do you remember me from school? Hullo Robert!"

Robert and Jimmy turned and were surprised to see their old friend standing there.

"Hi Aalap matey!" Robert said. "How's it hanging?"

"It is okay thank you matey. I have come late today."

"Where you living at the moment?" Robert asked.

"I am living at home matey." Aalap said. "Who are you?" He asked Sally.

"I am Sally. I am Jimmy's..." She still didn't know how to finish the sentence so she let it hang. But even so, it sounded about right.

"Oh. Hello. I have not had a girlfriend although I would like one. I have tried to go online dating but I have not yet met a girl."

"Okay!" Robert said. "You'll have to come round our house one day man, it's great!"

"You have a house too man? I am at my mum's house. You are all very lucky. Very lucky. Very lucky. All the people who went to our school I know don't have a house or a girlfriend or a boyfriend or a job."

"Yeah. We want jobs!" Robert said loudly, looking up the dark sky and punching the air.

"But you have a house. That is very cool man," Aalap said. "I think we have to go inside man. They are going to say what we are doing for Christmas man."

"Oh. Okay," Jimmy said, putting his hand gently on Sally's waist to steer her inside. *Maybe one day,* he thought, *he'd call Sally his girlfriend.* Without being scared she'd walk away or not talk to him again.

Back inside they took up their seats in the circle. Aalap came and joined them and they waited sipping drinks until Sophie stood up again, holding a pad of paper in her hands.

"Looks like we had a landslide victory guys!" She said and the chatter died away as they waited to hear what their project would be. "In third place with six votes was the bake sale and charity event. In second place with nine votes was the carol singing. So this year's project with a whopping eighteen votes is the party!" Whoops and cheers rose up from the group. "So, what we need now is to start thinking about how we want to do this? What we talked about before was doing cocktails and having music and inviting an extra person each as well, or even two. We think we can have a hundred people at the most. But we need to have a think about things like a theme and decorations and we need to allocate some jobs. Firstly, who would like to be head organizers?"

The panel who had spoken before instantly put their hands up and no one challenged them.

"Brilliant, sounds good. Now we need people to do decorations, music, costumes, filming, food... yes, Sally is it?"

"Jimmy will do filming as he is going to work with films," Sally said, lowering her hand.

Jimmy looked over to her, surprised and nervous suddenly. His heart rate had quickened when he heard filming mentioned but he was too nervous to put his own hand up.

"Is that right Jimmy?"

"Yes," Jimmy said. "I have a camera that I can use to do filming."

"Does anyone object, or is there anyone else who would like to do it?"

"I can help. It will be kick ass video!" Robert said. "I be his helper, right hand man, b...best friend!"

"Okay. That fine with everyone? Sally, would you like to make it three?"

"Make what three?"

"I mean help them, so there would be three people doing filming?"

"No thank you. I can help with food as I am a good cook."

"Okay. Jimmy and Robert doing filming, Sally doing food. I'll write the rest of the jobs down on paper up here and if you'd like to put your name under something, that'd be great. Then, chill for a bit, have a drink and we'll meet next week and really start planning. That okay with everyone?" She looked round at the nodding faces. "Excellent. Panel, anything more to say?"

"No thank you," Dan said.

"Okay then. Meeting adjourned," Sophie said, smiling. "Thank you for coming."

The assembled group dispersed from their circle and moved either into smaller circles or gravitated towards the bar. Jimmy, Sally and their new and old friends found themselves hanging around one corner of the room, taking turns to get the drinks and chatting away.

"Wh…wh… what… are y…y… you all do…doing … to…to…tomorrow?" Jason stammered towards the group, flapping his hand a bit as he did.

"We are going to do job getting," Lilly told him.

"Where are you going to get jobs man?" Aalap asked them.

"In the town. We are going to do small jobs until we can get jobs as a film man and a cook and a boss and a wrestler," Lilly said.

"Oh. Okay," Aalap said.

"That's brilliant!" Kyle said. "If you get jobs, can we have jobs too?"

"Do you not have jobs? Do you not have a support worker to help you do C.V so that you can give them to people who will then give you jobs?" Lilly asked.

"Yes," Gregory said. "But we have found job getting is very hard. There are not many jobs. I have been looking for a job for three years. I have applied to one hundred and thirty seven places. I have applied to shops and cafes and offices and supermarkets and libraries and everywhere. I have had a job for three months and two days in a supermarket. It was good there. I made four pounds an hour. But because it was work experience I wasn't allowed to work for very long, even though they said I was good."

"Oh. Okay," Lilly said.

"When we find jobs we will tell you where to find them," Sally said. "We have done a C.V and Duncan helped Jimmy do writing to films. We had a lady come and tell us what to do. She said we could do anything," she said, feeling her cheeks redden and letting her eyes dart between her friends to check they had missed the lie.

"Yeah, we'll get jobs!" Robert said loudly. "I'm going to be a wrestler one day. Look at my muscles!" He tensed his arms and smiled while they admired his growing biceps that were getting nicely toned at the gym.

"How do you become a wrestler man?" Aalap asked him.

"Well, dude… you get another job. And then you go to a wrestling match and show them how good you are then they give you a job. I will be the Undertaker's partner and we will put those other teams through the taaaaabbbbbllllleeeesss!"

"Oh. Okay dude," Aalap said. "I would like a job. I have been looking as well but it is very hard dude. Even when places say they are looking for people in the window the places are full and they have forgotten to take the signs down dude."

"Well, we are adults and adults go to work so we will get jobs and then tell you where jobs are and then the jobs will give us money in our bank account and we can save up and go on holiday," Lilly said.

"Excellent!" Kyle said. "Holidays are great! I love beaches!"

"Yes. Me too," said Lilly, looking up at Kyle.

At around nine O'clock people were starting to drift home. At half nine Duncan came and picked them up.

"Good time?" He asked them after they had said their good byes and climbed into the car.

"Yes. It was a very good time," Lilly said. "Jimmy is going to do filming at the event with Robert and me and Sally are going to do food and decorations. Kyle is going to do food and decorations as well. He is very happy and made me smile."

"Kyle?" Duncan asked, glancing surreptitiously into his rear view mirror at her.

"Yes. Kyle is someone we met at the club who is very nice and cool and I have his phone number," Lilly replied, squirming and staring down at the mat under her feet.

"Oh yeah?" Duncan said, smiling. "He sounds nice."

"He is nice," Lilly said. "I would like to see him again."

"Well maybe he should come round one day? Maybe he could come when we have our house-warming dinner party in a couple of weeks?"

"That would be nice!" Lilly said, letting her smile grow. "That would be very nice."

Back at the house they made themselves sandwiches and ate them in front of the television before the four younger adults went to bed at around half ten. When they'd gone Duncan went to the lounge, put on one of his favorite films, put his feet up and opened a bottle of beer. He was so involved in the film that he didn't hear the feet padding down the stairs and he barely noticed the figure come into the room.

"This film is Titanic?" Jimmy asked, coming in and sitting down on the arm chair.

"Jimmy! You made me jump," Duncan said, sitting up, slightly embarrassed by his choice of film.

"I don't like this bit. The man on the flag pole's life jacket disappears and then comes back again."

"You really don't like mistakes in films, do you mate?" Duncan asked.

"No. I like films, they are good. But mistakes make things not real."

"Yeah, fair enough. You okay? You went to bed ages ago."

"I am worried about tomorrow. We met some friends at club. They had been doing job finding for a long time but didn't get a job. But I know most people have got jobs. Do people not want to give jobs to us because of autism?"

Duncan sat up and turned to his young friend. He had never heard Jimmy be so open before, never heard him express any concerns about his moderate autism. There was the answer he wanted to give and the answer he should give, he knew that. And he almost said what he knew Jimmy wanted to hear. But the lad had been honest so he should be too, he decided.

"It's hard mate. People don't really understand about learning disabilities and it can often scare them off hiring you. What we've got to hope is that tomorrow you'll all be lucky enough to find somewhere that will see past the things you find hard, like handling money and customer service. And see instead that you're hard working, caring individuals with a hell of a lot to offer and even more to teach people."

"Oh. Okay," said Jimmy. "Do you think we will find someone like that?"

"I don't know mate. But all we can do is try, eh?"

"Okay."

"Good."

"Duncan, can I ask you something?"

"You can. I can't make any promises that I'll know the answer, but you can try."

"Okay. What does autism mean? It means it is hard to get a job. It used to mean I needed my hand held. It sometimes means people do not talk to me. It means I go to clubs with people with autism. But what is autism?"

Duncan looked at him and sighed. It was a difficult question and one not to be taken lightly, but how to explain?

"Jimmy, autism is a label. It is a name for people who have similar characteristics, who need similar help. People with autism can need any or all of the things you just said and more. Some people with autism find it hard to talk to people, some don't talk at all. Others talk okay. But everyone's different mate, everyone's an individual. Autism affects different people in different ways. Disabilities affect different people in different ways. The problem is, people are a bit... well... scared of the word autism, maybe because they don't understand it very well. I have dyslexia, but that's not the first thing people see when they see me, but it's a disability all the same. Most people have a disability of some sort; it's just not as obvious as yours. But although you've been diagnosed and labeled with autism which makes things difficult, it also means you get more help. Maybe without the label you would have got a job easier, but you wouldn't have me to help you shop and I know you find money difficult."

"Okay," said Jimmy. "I think I understand. I need some help with things and that is because I have autism? It means I am different and need different help?"

"Yes mate. But everyone's different to everyone else. And we've gotta do our best to get out there and show the world that people labeled as having 'disabilities' are just as valuable and have as much to offer as those who aren't."

"Okay," said Jimmy, nodding his head.

"And the most important thing to remember, the thing you should never, ever forget. Is that you are Jimmy Tiffin. You are Jimmy Tiffin who has been diagnosed with autism. You are not an autistic boy called Jimmy Tiffin. You understand the difference?"

"I am just me?"

"Exactly. Does that help?"

"Yes. Thank you."

"No problems mate. You want to watch the rest of the film with me?"

"No thank you. I will go to bed so I can rest and be ready for tomorrow."

"Fair play. Sweet dreams then mate."

"Thank you," Jimmy said, standing up. "I will go to sleep now."

And for the first time in a while, he fell asleep straight away. It was one of the best night's sleep he'd ever had, peaceful and pure, while Duncan sat downstairs with no real clue how much he'd just done for Jimmy.

5

On the bus into town none of the guys were speaking much.
Each had a plastic wallet with around fifteen CVs on their laps
and were holding them tightly. They were all staring out the
windows, ignoring the little looks and the hushed conversations they were used to. Mothers telling children not to look
or to comment about why the man's face was rounder and why
his eyes were slanted like they were. And why when they did
speak, did they speak in a strange way. All four were used to
this, although the anxiety, even in low levels, made these jour-
neys un-comfortable.

When they got into the centre of town, they got off the bus
and walked into the pedestrianized shopping street.

"Where shall we start?" Lilly asked them, as they stood in a
little huddle at the top of the high street.

"The lady said shops and cafes and supermarkets," Sally
said. "And restaurants so I can become a chef."

"Okay," Jimmy said.

They looked around them at the people rushing past, the busy shops and the buskers lining the streets.

"Let's go!" Robert said. But no one moved. All had felt their heart rates quicken, none had done this for real before.

"Right. We are adults and adults look for jobs. I like that shop over there I am going to go inside and I am going to ask for a job. It is a girl's clothes shop. Sally can come with me," Lilly said, pointing to a fashion shop across the way from them. "Let's go."

Lilly took Sally's arm and marched her across the street, through and around groups of people, trying to ignore the bustle and the noise. But once she reached the front of the shop, she stopped.

"It i..is b…busy. Maybe w…w…we should do this la…la…later," she said, turning.

"No," Sally said, "we should try. You like this shop. We should go in."

"Let's have a cig…cig…cigarette," Lilly said.

"No. After," Sally said, taking her friend's arm. "Let's try."

Sally started nudging Lilly into the shop, looking around, ignoring her racing heart, ignoring her palms that were sweating and marched them both towards an assistant who was hanging up clothes.

"Excuse me," Sally said. "Where do I go to get a job?"

"Sorry?" The pretty shop assistant said, raising a hand with pink nail extensions to her face, tapping the long nails on her cheek.

"Were do I go to get a job?" Sally repeated.

"I don't think they have jobs for people like you here," she said, pulling an ugly, thin smile.

"Where do I go to give my CV," Sally said, her cheeks burning but determined to push on.

The girl looked her up and down and pointed with her decorated nails, like a witch's, Sally thought, to a customer service desk near them.

"Okay," Sally said, but the girl had already turned back to her folding. She looked at her friend who had gone pale and realized for all Lilly's outward confidence, she was as nervous as the rest of them.

Still arm in arm Sally pulled Lilly over to the desk which was briefly and miraculously without a queue.

"How can I help you sweetie?" The lady behind the desk asked.

"We would like a job please. We have our C.V."

"Oh," said the woman of around thirty five, looking nervously around, wondering how close her manager was. She didn't, after all, want any discrimination law suit against her. "Well ladies, if you give me you C.V I'll be sure to get in touch if ever there is any positions opening up."

"Okay," said Sally smiling. "We would be very good at working with you." She opened up her plastic wallet and handed hers over to the lady. Shakily, Lilly did the same.

"Okay girls. Thanks for your interest and we'll be in touch."

"Thank you," Sally said. "I will look forward to you being in touch. Bye."

"Bye girls," the women said, breathing a sigh of relief as they left and scanning the crowds to try and work out which one of the eavesdroppers was the girl's carer, waiting to jump on her if she didn't give them an equal chance or if she put *one* foot out of line. *Probably have no problems getting a job.* She thought as the girls left. *Took me weeks to find this one. Positive discrimination, bet they end up getting paid twice what I'm getting here and that's on top of benefits. Bloody Government.*

She put the C.V's under the desk, making a mental note to tell everyone what had happened and to make sure they stick with the same story if the girls came back in. She was sure everyone would agree. They didn't want to be clearing up after a couple of girls with disabilities, on top of their already demanding jobs. Didn't get paid nearly enough for that kind of thing.

Back out on the street, Lilly lit up a cigarette with shaking hands.

"Did you get a job?" Jimmy asked them.

"N...n...not yet," Lilly said, trying desperately to meet Jimmy's eyes. "It is very e...easy to ask though. They will call us."

"Oh. Okay," Jimmy said. "There is a video shop over there. I would like to do asking in there."

"Okay," Sally said. "Let's go."

At the video rental shop, Robert and Jimmy went in leaving Lilly to finish her cigarette with Sally.

Three minutes later they came back.

"Did you do job getting in there?" Sally asked.

"They will let us know if there are any jobs to be had," Jimmy said.

"But the sign in the window says there are jobs?" Lilly said pointing.

"Yes. That is an old sign that they haven't taken down. They will let us know if any jobs come up," Jimmy said, trying to keep his head up. After all, he would soon get replies from the film companies; they would give him a job.

"Okay," Sally said. "Shall we go to the café over there?"

"Okay," Jimmy said, "let's go."

They looked around the town for three hours, stopping just once for a foamy, chocolate latte and a muffin. Each had handed over all their CVs and each could recite the mantra from heart. 'There are no positions available at the moment, but if you leave your CV, we'll be in touch.'

"We can try the other town tomorrow maybe?" Lilly said, breathing a sigh of relief as they boarded the bus and began the journey home. "It is not very far from our house."

"Yes. Maybe they will have more jobs that are available. If not, we can just wait for them to call us," said Sally.

"Yeah, plan dudes!" Robert said. "We can try tomorrow and wait for interviews."

"Okay," Lilly said, "we will get jobs soon and then we can save money and go on holiday."

"Yeah! And when I'm a wrestler I can take you to shows and you can watch."

"That would be very good," Lilly said. "We will do that if Jimmy can get a break from filming and I can from being a boss and Sally can from being a chef."

"Yes," Said Robert, "if you can get a break."

6

Jimmy was sitting on the sofa looking down at the letter that was on the table, signed by George Farrington, CEO of 'Showdown Pictures.' He had some difficulty reading but since this was his fourth, he had become quite good at recognizing rejection letters when he saw them. He wasn't certain though and this was the one he really wanted, this was 'Showdown Pictures.' As the other rejection letters had come in, he hadn't been so worried. But this one, this one was making him shake. His friends were all in their rooms, sleeping in. They had spent the last two weeks getting up early and traipsing around nearby towns and shops, desperate to find somewhere, chasing up old applications, doing all the things the lady from 'Work Now' had told them to do. But they had, had no luck. Nothing. Today was their day off. Today was going to be a good day, today they were hosting their first ever dinner party and they were all excited, getting to do what they had seen their parents do on a number of occasions. Getting to do being adults.

Feet on the stairs meant someone was up.

"Morning Jimmy," Duncan said, used now to the young man getting up at seven fifteen every morning. "How are you?"

"Duncan! I have a letter from Showdown. Can you help me with reading please?"

"Sure can mate," Duncan said, steeling himself for yet another disappointment. He sat down next to Jimmy and picked up the letter, giving it a quick scan first. "Right then mate. It says thank you very much for your letter. Unfortunately we don't hire anyone without previous film experience. Please accept our apologies. And please accept these free tickets to our tour that you can use whenever you like." He turned to Jimmy and smiled. "Sorry mate. Not this time."

"But that is okay," Sally said from the doorway making the others jump. "Jimmy is doing filming for the party at club. That is experience."

"That's right!" Duncan said. "Once you've done that, we can try again. When they see how good it's going to be, maybe you can get a job after that."

"Okay," said Jimmy who'd been close to tears. "We can try again."

"Good thinking Sally. But what you doing up so early?"

"I need to do shopping and getting ready for doing cooking."

"The dinner party's not until seven though; you've got eleven hours to go."

"Yes. But Jimmy's parents are coming. And Robert's parents. And Kyle and Gregory from the club. And Lilly's mum. I have a lot to do."

"Can we help?" Duncan asked.

"Yes. We need to do shopping. We need a car as it will be too heavy to carry on a bus."

"Well, the shops don't open for an hour. Let's grab some breakfast first, eh?"

"Okay," said Sally. "I will have toast."

Robert was the next to come down.

"Sorry Jimmy," he said once he'd heard the news. "You will be in films soon!"

"Okay," Jimmy said. "I will get experience and I will try again."

"Did you see you had a letter as well, Robert?" Duncan asked, passing him an envelope which Robert opened up quickly.

"It says that I should come in to see... Um, I can't see this word."

"You want a hand?" Duncan asked.

"Yes please," Robert said, "my eyes not working too well today."

Duncan scanned it quickly.

"It says you've got an interview!" He almost shouted. "At the men's fashion store, 'Sergio Taylor.' Well done mate, that's a posh place."

"Yes!" Robert shouted, jumping out of his seat and punching the air.

"Well done," Jimmy said, smiling, feeling only small pangs of envy.

"Yes that is good," Sally said, feeling bigger pangs, but trying to be happy for him.

"I will call my mum!" Robert said. "Can you dial for me please Duncan?"

"No probs mate. Let's write the date on the calendar first, eh?"

"Yeah! Let's do it!" Robert said.

Lilly got up just in time to join them in the supermarket run. They had already made a list of all the things they were going to need. Sally was making Spaghetti Bolognese for most, pasta and tomato sauce for Lilly's vegetarian mum, and for all; garlic bread, tomato and mozzarella salad and chocolate mousse. She had spent a happy evening searching dinner party ideas online until she found recipes she was confident with and thought that everyone would like. Recipes that also came with step by step pictures.

When they got in from the supermarket Sally took the food into the kitchen and laid it all out on the counters whilst the other four set about cleaning the house to 'parent and guest' standards. In the kitchen Sally arranged the four recipes on the table along with the schedule her and Duncan had made up. First, the schedule said, make the chocolate mousse and put it in the fridge to set. By this instruction was written eleven O'clock. It was half past ten now, so she set out the ingredients. Following the recipe, she separated ten eggs and put the yolks in one bowl and the whites in another. She then broke the dark chocolate up into large chunks and put it into another large bowl. She measured up the butter and put that to one side. Next she put some water in a saucepan on the gas hob then put the bowl with the chocolate in it over the saucepan. Once the ramekins were set up, she sat back and watched her watch. When it ticked onto eleven she started making the mousse so that it could be stored in the fridge, ready and waiting for after dinner.

As the hours ticked on Sally got more and more nervous. She hadn't seen Jimmy's parents for a while and they had never seemed keen on her. She tried her best to concentrate on the cooking, to take her mind off things, wanting it to be the best it could be. By the time six O'clock rolled by, everything was going smooth. Mousses were in the fridge and all the ingredients were set out and ready for cooking at seven, as the schedule suggested. The table was set, the white wines and beers were cooling in the fridge, the three bottles of red on the side, one was opened with a glass or two already slyly drunk between the five of them. Now all she had to do was wait.

At seven on the dot she started cooking, softly frying the onions and the mince. At the same time the door bell went. Jimmy, who'd been sitting in the kitchen at the beautifully laid table, jumped up to go to the door but was beaten by Robert and Lilly who'd been in the lounge. Robert opened the door.

"Gregory and Kyle. My guys!" He said loudly, slapping their hands.

"Hi mate! This is excellent!" Kyle said, holding a bottle of Chilean red. "Hi Lilly, you look lovely tonight! Very lovely!"

"Thank you. I like your pink shirt it is very smart."

"Thank you! It's pink, I love pink, it's my favorite."

"Mine too," said Lilly. "Would you like to come in and have a drink in the lounge where we have also put olives and crisps and dips into bowls for people to eat before dinner?"

"Y...yes please," said Gregory.

"Sounds excellent!" Said Kyle, beaming his huge smile at them all, before turning to wave at the support worker who'd driven them, who waved then set off to his home.

In the lounge Kyle and Gregory sat while Lilly got them a beer each. Jimmy didn't have time to say two words as the door bell went again. Him and Robert got up and answered it together.

"Hello love. Hello Robert," Jimmy's mum said smiling. "Don't you guys look smart. Here you are darling," she added handing him a bottle of coke and one of lemonade.

"Thank you. Hello mum. Hello dad. Come in please," Jimmy said, taking the bottles and leading them though to the lounge.

"Hello there!" Kyle said as they came in, standing to shake their hands. "I'm Kyle and this is Gregory."

"Hi guys," said Jimmy's dad shaking their hands.

"Would you like a drink Mr and Mrs Tiffin?" Lilly asked. "We have beer and white wine and red wine or soft drinks."

"Oh," said Mrs Tiffin, raising her eyebrows in Duncan's direction. "Sounds like you have a lot of alcohol here?"

"We are all over eighteen and we have identification," said Lilly. "We are adults and adults can drink and we have identification."

"I guess so," Mrs Tiffin said, not convinced. "I'll just have a coke please for the moment."

"It's alright, I'll drive home," Mr Tiffin said. "I'll have a beer and my wife will have a large glass of white wine. Where's Sally by the way?"

"She is doing the cooking as she is going to be a chef when she's older," Lilly told them.

"Is she doing that on her own?" Mrs Tiffin asked eyes widening, glancing towards the kitchen as if expecting smoke to be billowing out into the hallway.

"Yes," Lilly said.

"My wife just means, would she like company, I'm sure," Jimmy's dad said quickly. "Let's go and say hi, shall we dear?"

"Let's," his mum said unsure and they got up and headed towards the kitchen.

Sally nearly dropped the big metal pan full of boiling water and spaghetti when the kitchen door suddenly opened and she saw Jimmy's mum and dad step in.

"Are you okay?" Mrs Tiffin said quickly, jumping forward to grab the pan that Sally was holding.

"Yes. You surprised me, so I nearly dropped it but it is okay because I didn't," Sally answered.

"I can't believe they're making you do this all by yourself, what if you hurt yourself?"

"Darling..." Mr Tiffin tried,

"No, I'm serious. We can all go pretending this is perfectly normal if we like and it's all fun and games but that's a pan full of boiling water, she could have been badly scalded..."

"Mrs Tiffin, it is..."

"It's okay Sally. Would you like me to finish up in here?" She said, moving over to the hob to stir the mince."

"Mrs Tiffin..."

"You did your best Sally, but there are some things you just..."

"Mrs Tiffin, I am a very good cook, I cook for my mum all the time and I am good! Please go and sit down, I am an adult. You are guest. It is rude to go into someone's kitchen and start doing cooking with not asking!" Sally shouted, hands clenched by her side.

Mrs Tiffin looked at her. Then she looked around the room at the rota they'd made, the beautifully laid kitchen table, the food that looked, well, like it should look and she took a step back.

"I'm…I'm sorry Sally," she said quietly, "you're right. Look at all this food. And this clean house. I guess you are an adult, eh? I… it's just that I always thought… never mind. Where's that glass of wine?"

"There is wine in the fridge," Sally said, "I will make you a glass."

The dinner itself went perfectly. The food was expertly cooked; conversation and wine were flowing; freer and freer with each top-up. Everybody was laughing and getting along well.

In the lounge, sitting with coffee and the fair trade mint chocolates that Lilly's mum had brought, they rounded off the evening nicely.

Jimmy looked over at his mum who had a warm glow about her that made him happy to see. She was chatting to Sally about recipes and food and both looked engaged. For the first time he saw his mum as just someone like him, like all of them, just humans doing what they thought was best, living how they thought they should. Trying to be adults. Maybe no one really knew how?

When eleven rolled by Jimmy's dad had to positively tear his mum away from the conversation she was having with Lilly; who was disappointed that Kyle had had to leave early because his carer, who'd picked him up, didn't work past ten.

"There'll be other times love," she was saying, giving them a wink.

"Come on, let's go, Monday tomorrow," Mr Tiffin said for the third time.

"Okay. Right everyone, we're going to go. But before we do I'd like to say thank you to our chef, Sally, the food was excellent. And to all of you for being such good hosts and for looking a..." She stopped, her head dropped and she sighed. "Sorry. For being such good friends to my Jimmy," she continued, raising her head once more.

"Bye Mum, bye Dad," Jimmy said, going over to give them both a brief hug. "I will call you soon."

"Okay Jimmy, we'll look forward to it," his dad said.

"Bye Sally," his mum said giving her a quick kiss on the cheek, "you're doing great."

"Bye Mrs Tiffin," Sally said.

"Please," she said, "call me Penny."

7

They had all become very used to the bus journey, having done it at least twice a week for the last month. But this time there was an air of excitement about them. This time Robert had an interview, their first since they'd started looking those four weeks and three days ago. Everything else, every other CV handed in, every other written letter (Jimmy had written five more times to different places,) or phone calls had amounted to nothing at all.

Robert was wearing a black suit over a white shirt and red tie, all bought for him by his Dad just for the occasion. He had done mock interviews with Duncan and had researched all about the shop online. He was as ready as he ever would be. He had some work experience in clothes shops that had been set up by his school some time ago and this, he'd rightly presumed, was the reason he was getting the interview. It would be a good job too, seven pounds fifty an hour to work on the shop floor, tidying, serving, stocking. He wasn't a wrestler, not yet. But he loved wearing the suit, carrying his file with all his information it, just like all the other working adults around. He already felt like he had made it.

When they got into town, Jimmy, Sally and Lilly hugged their friend and said good luck, before crossing the road to go and sit in a small, independent coffee shop opposite 'Sergio Taylor's' to wait. Robert turned to face the shop, straightened his tie, checked himself in the plain glass of this fashionable store, breathed deep then went on inside.

"Can I help you?"The man behind the registers said.

"My name is Robert Randall and I'm here for an interview," Robert said, extending his hand to the man who gave him a sideways look but took it.

"Okay. I'll call up to the managers," the assistant said, before heading out a door in the back of the shop to a phone just on the other side.

"Yep, Robert is here Mr Bertie.Yep, okay, I'll send him up. There's something… it's, don't worry, you'll see. Okay I'll send him up."The man came back through the door and smiled at Robert, not realizing he could be heard through the door.

"Right you are mate, come this way. Take the stairs to the next floor and it's the door straight ahead."

"Thank you very much," Robert said, making a motion a little like a bow.

Upstairs Robert steadied himself again briefly before he opened the door marked office. Inside was a large, plush room with a long wooden table at one end, behind which sat three men, who gave Robert a slightly quizzical look as he entered.

"Hi, can we help?" The one in the middle wearing a smart black suit asked.

"Yes. My name is Robert and I am here for an interview."

"You're Robert?" The man asked. His face scrunched briefly before he professionally ironed it out. "Fantastic, please come in and take a seat." He motioned to the seat in front of him.

"Thank you," said Robert, feeling disorientated. Duncan said they would shake his hand first. Should he initiate it? Or should he just sit? The confusion meant he ended up hovering above the chair.

"Please, sit," the man in the middle said. So Robert sat. "My name's Oliver Bertie. And these are my colleagues Neil and David..."

"Pleasure to meet you," Robert said, smiling back at their smiles. Already he could feel something was wrong.

"Do you, um... have anyone with you at all today?" The man introduced as David asked.

"My friends are waiting for me in the café."

"The one across that road? Great place that one," said David, speaking slowly and methodically. Patronizingly.

"Now, you're here for the job of sales assistant?" Oliver said, still wearing that half smile, head still cocked slightly, speaking as slow as his colleague just had. And suddenly Robert could feel it. He tried telling himself that this was how all interviews were done. But it didn't help. He could feel his features, his rounded face, his thin eyes, his smaller physical form, start becoming more and more pronounced. He could feel every feature about him that was different grow, throb and twist, become contorted and ugly until his disability became him. Because that's all they could see, he realized. They weren't seeing Robert with his resume, his hard working attitude, his learned skills and his good nature. They were seeing Robert the man with Down's syndrome. And they weren't going to make the effort to look past it.

He tried to steel himself but his answers weren't flowing like they did in practice. He kept tripping over words, mumbling, saying things wrong. All he could think was that they hadn't realized he had disability. Tears were forming behind his eyes that were hard to keep hidden

When the interview was done he practically ran out of the room. They hadn't listened to a word he'd said, he knew that. By about half-way through he'd been expecting the outcome, which was naturally; 'we're looking for someone with more experience.' And as soon as the door was shut, he let the tears flow. He ran down the short staircase into the shop then right out the entrance. He couldn't understand why they hadn't listened. It had taken him a month of trying to get one interview at one shop and they hadn't listened to a word.

Was this how it was always going to be, he wondered, *was this it?*

He didn't stop crying until he was back in his house, in his room lying face down on the bed. If he couldn't even get a job like that, what chance as a wrestler did he have? He thought as he put the pillow over the back of his head and held it down over his ears, trying to block out as much of the unfair world as he possibly could.

8

Spirits in the house were low. Sally was in the kitchen making a dinner of chicken nuggets and chips for everyone. Robert had barely left his room in the last week, not really eating, not going to any of the clubs he'd signed up for, not even going to the gym which worried them all the most. Lilly was doing her best, but rejection after rejection in town was leaving her tired. And Jimmy had just received another rejection letter from a film company, his thirteenth.

"When you have done filming at the event, you can get a job at filming," Sally said, loading the baking tray with chips.

"Okay. But if they don't want to see me, how can I show them?"

"We could do the tour at Showdown Picture Film Company and show them."

"I don't think people with autism can get jobs and do working and be adults," Jimmy said, letting his head rest on his arms which were crossed on the kitchen table.

"We have to try," Sally said, moving over to him to rest her hand on his arm.

"Why?" Said Jimmy sitting up.

"We do," said Sally quietly.

"Okay," said Jimmy as quietly. "Okay."

When they had eaten they set off for the club for another meeting and evening of organizing followed by a mini-disco. The car was unusually quiet for the drive, even Duncan was tired following just under two months of reading rejection letters out to the guys he'd become attached to.

"Right, see you back here at ten?"

"Okay," Lilly said, "we will see you later Duncan after the club has finished."

"Later's guys," Duncan said before turning his car around and heading home for a quiet evening with 'Love Actually' and a couple of beers.

They went inside together, not waiting for Lilly to finish her cigarette who had to stub it out half smoked on the pavement. Inside the chairs were already set out. Aalap was waiting for them, hanging around in one corner of the circle.

"Hello dudes," he said as they took their places. "How are you dudes?"

"Okay," Lilly said.

"Yeah, we're okay mate," Robert said.

"That's good mate," Aalap said. "That is good."

The meeting lasted about an hour as they ran through the different bits and bobs, costumes, entertainers, invites, foods and other details. For half an hour they split into their groups to organize their separate bits. Robert and Jimmy sat together as the film crew, though there wasn't much to talk about since they had the camera, Jimmy knew how to work it and Robert was going to interview people. They had already come up with a list of questions to ask. Jimmy wasn't that interested that day anyway, not after another rejection. *If people wouldn't even talk to me, what was the point of all this?* He couldn't help but think.

Once the organizing bits were done, a DJ started up and people started dancing. The bar was steadily a few people deep and since conversation wasn't exactly flowing, the guys including Aalap, Kyle, Gregory and Jason, just stayed near the bar drinking.

"Lilly, do you like dancing? I like dancing. Dancing is great. Dancing together is great too!" Kyle said to her, eliciting her first real smile of the evening.

"Yes, I would like to do dancing with you please," she said.

He stepped out in front and offered her his hand which she took with a grin and let him lead her out into the dance floor where they faced each other and bopped away.

"Shall we do dancing?" Sally asked Jimmy who was sipping a vodka and coke.

"No thank you," Jimmy said, looking away, tapping his foot to the music.

"Oh. Okay," said Sally. "But I would like to dance with you Jimmy."

"No thank you Sally," Jimmy repeated.

"Okay," Sally said.

"I…I…I will dance with you plea…ea…se Sa…Sa… Sally," Jason said to her. Sally looked over at Jimmy who had started talking to one of the girls, Justine.

"Okay," Sally said, glancing back once at Jimmy before letting Jason take her hand and lead her to the dance floor.

When they got there, Sally let Jason put his hand around her waist and take her other hand in his so they could dance to the rhythm and blues that the DJ was playing. She kept glancing back at Jimmy who was still talking to Justine. She wished he was here with her.

Jimmy and Justine were deep in conversation about the party.

"Are you looking forward to the party?" Jimmy asked.

"I…I do parties and dancing yeah," Justine said. "I like music like rap and things and pop. Are you filming? Are you a film director? I would like to be on TV. Can you make sure you film me at the party?"

"Yes. I am doing filming and can film you," Jimmy said.

"Do you have a girlfriend?" Justine asked. "I would like a boyfriend."

"I have…" Jimmy started looking around and for the first time clocked Sally and Jason. Shivers ran down his spine, he stared for a moment at the hand that was on her waist and the other that was in his hand and felt pangs in his stomach that hurt.

"Do you have a girlfriend?" Justine asked again, as Jimmy thought about how his hand was on her delicate waist.

"No," Jimmy said simply.

"Would you like a cigarette outside?" Justine asked.

"Yes," Jimmy said.

By the time Sally looked around again, she just had time to see the two of them heading out the back door together.

By the time ten rolled around, Sally was tired from all the dancing. Aalap, Kyle, Jason and Gregory had gone already and it was just Sally, Robert and Lilly of their group left. Jimmy had not re-appeared after heading out with Justine.

"Shall we go to see Duncan?" Lilly asked.

"Okay," Sally said, softly.

"Where's Jimmy?" Robert asked.

"He went outside with a girl," Sally said.

"Oh. Were they talking?"

"I don't know," said Sally, now fighting back a few tears.

They said their goodbyes and put their empty glasses at the bar.

"Are you okay?" Lilly asked; linking arms now with Sally, both were stumbling slightly.

"Yes. I am okay. Are you okay? How was Kyle?"

"He kissed me," Lilly said grinning. "It was nice. It was wet and cold and I did not think it would be cold but it was nice because you kiss someone when you like someone and he kissed me. I want to see him again. I would like him to be my boyfriend."

"Okay," Sally said.

"Why were you dancing with Jason?" Robert asked.

"He asked me to."

"Why were you not dancing with Jimmy?"

"He said no," Sally said, focusing on walking straight as they moved through the exit into the car park.

Outside Duncan's car was already there. Jimmy was also there, sitting in the front seat. He didn't look at them as they came over, his eyes were closed and he was leaning his head into the rest. He didn't even look up when the car door were opened as the guys got in.

"Good night guys?" Duncan asked.

"It was good," Lilly said, smiling.

"Yeah? Kyle there, was he?"

"Yes. Kyle was there." She giggled which made Duncan smile.

"Good," he said. "And you Robert? Sally?"

"It was good," Robert said.

"Yes," Sally said, with no conviction.

When they got home everyone went to bed; everyone apart from Sally and Jimmy who went into the lounge, both knowing that something needed to be said. The atmosphere in the room was thick. Both had so much to say but found it so hard to say it. They sat both staring at the floor for twenty minutes, Jimmy clenching his fists and Sally tapping her fingers rapidly on her thigh.

"I am going to go to bed," Jimmy said eventually.

"No," Sally said simply.

"Why?"

"Because. Why did you go with Justine?"

"I don't know. I didn't want to see you and Jason," Jimmy said, after a pause.

"Oh," Sally said. How could she make him see? She had so much to say to him, so much she wished he would realize. But he didn't get it.

"Please would you come with me please?" Sally said, standing up and offering a hand to Jimmy which he reluctantly took.

She led him upstairs and into her room. Sally's room was big, decorated in many shades of purple, with a wooden wardrobe and desk both cluttered with things.

"Jimmy," she said softly. "I get upset a lot. But when I am upset there is one thing that makes me happy," she said, sitting down on the bed and drawing back the covers. "It is this," she said picking up the picture of them sat together at the restaurant on Jimmy's fifteenth birthday. "Your mum sent it to me after your party."

Jimmy picked it up and ran a finger across the glossy picture, barely recognizing the young man and woman before him.

"Sally," he said, quietly, sitting down next to her, "why is life hard? I want to be a film director but I can't do that. I want to be an adult but I can't do getting a job or being social or driving. I want you to be my girlfriend but I don't want that to go bad."

"Jimmy. You should be a film man. And when you have done your filming people will see this. You are good but people are stupid. I'm not stupid. I want to do being your girlfriend and do kissing and..."

She didn't have time to finish. Jimmy put his hand on her waist and leant in to kiss her. Suddenly they were falling back together on the bed, kissing deeply and rolling around. Then, to both their surprises, they were touching each other where neither had been touched by someone else before, taking each other clothes off, experiencing each other and feelings, emotions, sensations neither had felt before. The only moment of clarity Jimmy had was when he stopped to go and get the protection that was in the bottom of his cupboard.

When he had come back, he put it on with some difficulty. But once it was on, he laid back down next to Sally who was now naked and slowly, awkwardly, but perfectly they had sex for the first time.

When they had finished, Sally lay with her head in the crook of Jimmy arm, smiling. Jimmy was lying back on the bed, smiling as well. Neither had known they could feel this good, this safe, this secure. They didn't have to say anything, didn't have to try. All they had to do was be, right there with each other. Exactly where they both wanted to be. Happy. Adults. Together.

9

Jimmy was standing with another rejection letter in his hand. This was his worst type, nothing was personal, it was just a standard letter. But he wasn't worried. Today was the day of the party. Today was the day he would prove he was great with a camera. He'd be sure to get a job then. Sally believed in him and that meant everything.

For the past few weeks he had woken up with her every morning, and he was sure she got more and more beautiful. Or maybe, he conceded, he just saw her in different ways and each one was as beautiful as the next. Sometimes for instance, she woke up and some of her hair was stuck to her face. Or some of her make up had smudged. Or her eyes had dark marks under them. Each time, she was so beautiful.

They were proper boyfriend and girlfriend now. They held hands all the time and kissed whenever they felt like it. Jimmy hadn't used his bed or his bedroom in a long time.

That's why the rejection hadn't got him like the others. He'd make it. He could do anything while he was with her.

And on top of this, tonight he was getting the experience that 'Showdown pictures' told him he needed. Tonight would be notch number one in his portfolio.

They were all pretty excited, they needed this day. They had spent months planning and it was finally here. This was their day, they were a part of it and it was going to run smoothly; they'd make sure of it.

They drove to the community centre at half past twelve to start setting up. They pulled up in one of the few empty spaces left and all five clambered out. Duncan popped the boot open and Jimmy went round to take the handheld camera, tripod and microphone out of the back.

Inside the place was already buzzing, people were stringing up decorations of all sorts on the walls and hanging things on the Christmas tree in the corner; Instantly all four of them regretted not being here sooner.

"Hi!" Sophie called over to them.

"Hi, we are here for the setting up of the party," Lilly said to her.

"Brilliant. Now, you two were on food, right?"

"Yes," Sally and Lilly answered.

"Excellent. If you want to head to the kitchen then, you can get started there. Gill is in charge of delegating, she'll let you know what needs to be done. You guys are doing the filming, yes?"

"Yes," said Jimmy on behalf of himself and Robert. "We need to start setting up now so that we can do an introduction of setting up and do some interviews before it starts and then we can edit it later," he added feeling the excitement begin to well up. Here he was, a real director, telling people what needs to be done.

"Okay then. Well we thought Paul could support you with that, he's one of our new workers who's done a film course at college."

"Oh," said Jimmy deflating a bit, "that is okay."

In the kitchen, an hour later, Sally was showing Lilly how to make mini quiches, using short curst pastry. She had shown off her cooking skills before when making cakes and other bits on club nights, so she was given quite a bit of leeway to go for it and a lot of space in which to spread herself out across the work surfaces. Lilly was listening to her every word and trying to follow he every movement, but her pastry kept falling apart and her fillings didn't look as neat. Sally eventually gave up and put her onto mixing duty and did the other preparations herself.

Jimmy and Robert had set up the camera and were looking down their lists at the people who needed to be interviewed about the party. They started off with one of the head board members, Daniel.

"Hi Dan," Jimmy said from behind the camera.

"Hi Jimmy and Robert," Dan said towards the camera.

"Can you tell us about the party?"

"Yes. We are having a party. It is for our club. It will be fun and there is decorations and punch and food."

"Okay. Thank you," said Jimmy.

"That is okay. No problems pal," Dan said, sauntering off back to the Christmas tree.

"Who's next Robert?" Jimmy asked once he'd gone.

"We need to interview the board members and Sophie and some other people," Robert said, checking his list that was attached to a wooden clipboard.

"Okay. Can you please go and get Sophie?"

"On my way boss Jimmy!"

When the setting up was done, everyone dispersed to go home and get changed.

Back at their house, all four went to their separate rooms to put on their hired clothes for the evening. Jimmy had got a tuxedo, as had Robert; Lilly and Sally had hired long, flowing dresses from the high street on one of their happier trips down that road.

Sally and Lilly were scurrying around upstairs still, while the ready and waiting boys sat in the sitting room.

"You both look like James Bond," Duncan said coming into the room with three beers.

"Which one?" Jimmy asked.

"Don't know mate. All of them."

"Oh. Okay. You look very nice as well."

"Thank you," said Duncan, who was wearing a suit as well; ready to enjoy the night with his guys. "You sure you don't mind me coming?"

"We're allowed to bring friends!" Robert said, smiling.

"Thanks," said Duncan sincerely, "that means a lot to me guys."

By the time they'd sipped their way through a Budweiser each, the girls had begun to make their way down the stairs. When they got through the door, Jimmy turned to look at his girl and his jaw dropped straight open. She had curled her hair with Lilly's help and it was bouncing around her bare shoulders. Her dress was blue and floor length, made of silk, loose around her waist but tighter around her chest, with no straps. He wanted to say something, knew he should, but no words could come out, not even a murmur. Sally smiled at this, smiled at him in his Tuxedo and a moment passed between the two of them that the other three felt shoot down their spines.

"You two look great!" Duncan said; the first to speak.

"Yeah!" Robert said.

"Thank you," said Lilly. "You three look very nice as well."

They got back to the club house at seven and Duncan was told to stay in the car for half an hour while they finished setting up. The fire breathing, juggling, magician they'd hired for the night was standing outside, having a cigarette, so they stepped past him and went on in.

It looked even better than how they'd left it. The lights in the hall were off now and the disco lights and mirror ball were on, throwing freckled light across the walls, floor and ceiling. All four had stopped by the door way, looking at the long table of food and drink around one side, the tinsel, the lights, the happy Christmas banner, the DJ booth and the groups milling around putting final touches to everything. Jimmy raised the camera and took a panoramic shot of the whole scene, emptier now than it would be so you could see everything they'd worked so hard to set up. He ended the shot on the six foot Christmas tree piled high with baubles and paper, homemade decorations. It was a good shot that would end up as the opening one once he and Paul had done the edit.

He kept filming as Sally, Lilly and a few others started bringing out even more trays of food: mini quiches, mini pizzas, mini pasties along with the bowls of crisps and cocktail sausages on sticks. Lilly and Sally waved at the camera as they passed and Robert waved back. Some of the others smiled, some frowned, some ignored it but all got filmed.

At seven-thirty Duncan came in, the first guest so he was made a fuss of as Emily, one of the other service users, draped flowers around his neck and he suffered four people asking him if he wanted a drink. He took a glass of punch then went and stood by the tables, helping himself to cocktail sausages and crisps. It took another half hour for it to really fill up, most support workers, parents or friends came around eight, arriving in pairs or in groups. Social workers were served mini-quiches and made appropriate cooing noises, parents and friends in jaunty Santa hats and flowers around their necks, sipped punch and shared a joke or two. The DJ interspersed his usual music with Christmas classics and everyone danced, or laughed and smiled at the dancers, told jokes or watched the magician perform his tricks.

Kyle asked Lilly to dance again and they shared their second kiss to 'White Christmas' in the middle of the dance floor and everyone just smiled or averted their eyes. Sally stayed replenishing the food and enjoyed hearing all the nice things that were being said about it all.

Robert chatted up one girl, Emily, and got a kiss from her then went and chased two of the prettier support workers, coming back to his filming duties every now and then.

Jimmy, on the other hand, only put down the camera twice. Once to put his arms around his best friends and jump up and down to Slade's classic, 'I Wish It Could Be Christmas Every Day;' and once to pull Sally in close to him and dance with her slowly under the mistletoe to 'Last Christmas' kissing her softly, passionately and then intensely as the song drew to a close.

When the lights came on at the end of the night and after everyone had said how good things went and how great it all was, they piled back into Duncan's car, who drove the five of them home.

"You guys enjoy it as much as you looked like you were?" He asked, glancing first next to him and then in the mirror.

"It was great," Lilly said yawning.

"The best night ever," Jimmy said. "Second best," he added after catching a look from Sally.

10

Jimmy was smiling and he had every right to. He was on a train, holding his girlfriend's hand, on his way to 'Showdown Pictures,' clutching to him his camera that held all the film that would make or break him; that he had spent the last week editing with Paul. And more than this, they had done this themselves. They had gotten the train times off the internet, with minimal help from Duncan, boarded the right train, written down a schedule; a list of the things they needed to do and the directions they needed to get to the studio. It was an amalgamation of everything; all the little pieces, all the things they had learnt, everything since he'd written his dreams in that little thought bubble at school, to now. This is what it was all about.

He was nervous, shaking as stops fell away and he counted them down, one by one in his head, mentally ticking them off, picturing the whole route in his mind.

Sally squeezed his hand, then leant over and gave him a kiss on the cheek. No one gasped, no one looked, no one told them to stop, no one was even watching which was a whole new thing for them. They truly were all grown up.

They got off at Charring Cross station and checked their directions. Once they'd found the right exit, they were off, walking quickly and purposefully, not looking about at the lunch time traffic which had almost ground to a halt along the main street.

They reached the building just a few minutes later, a modern looking place made of brick and glass, three stories high and went through the double doors and up to the reception desk.

"I would like to see the manager about getting a job," Jimmy said, as confidently as he could. "I have experience," he added, waving his camera in his hand.

"Do you have an appointment?" A man wearing a red sports jacket and a gold framed name badge that announced him as Bill asked.

"No, but I have a letter that said I need experience and I have now got experience," Jimmy said, handing over the letter which Bill glanced at.

"Well, I'm afraid the head of production is busy all day today. You have to call up and get an appointment."

"We did but they said he had no time."

"Oh well, try again. You're more then welcome to go on our tour, have a look around the history of our studios if you'd like? It says here you can have a free look around, that's pretty good."

"Oh. Okay then," said Jimmy, who had thought this could be the way of things. He wasn't worried though, all he had to do was find someone high enough up to see his film. Then surely they would hire him.

"Okay. If you go through those doors over by the cabinet over there, they lead into our little museum. Ok guys? We have quizzes and puzzles to do on the way round if you're interested?"

"No, thank you," Sally said, "we are twenty-three years old."

"Okay," Bill said, turning to try and disguise his embarrassment.

They went over to the doors and walked on through, purposefully, both their hearts racing as they moved into the rooms. The museum or 'tour' itself was nothing more than two adjacent rooms, filled with photos of people on film sets or famous people posing with cameras and the film crew, along with a few glass cases with miniature sets inside them. There were a few wall-mounted screens which played you short clips and adverts for their newest films if you touched the illuminated buttons and although Jimmy didn't want to, he walked straight past them all.

"This way," Sally said, taking Jimmy's free hand and pulling him to a door at the back marked 'no entry.' She pushed on it and it opened outwards. They both froze, waiting for maybe an alarm or a security guard but nothing happened. The door had opened to a corridor; one direction led back towards reception, the other led to a staircase. They went for the staircase. Gingerly, they took the stairs one by one, running their hands up the long, metal handrail, looking around, waiting to be stopped.

'*You have to take a chance.*'

This is what each director or film maker Jimmy had seen interviewed said at some point during the many documentaries he had watched. And this is what he told himself as he and Sally reached the first floor landing. He could feel the sweat beads building on his forehead and dream or no dream, he knew he would've turned back had Sally not been there, pulling him along by his hand.

"I think we should go up to the next floor," Sally said, ignoring the door in front of them and pulling Jimmy to the next set of stairs.

"Okay," said Jimmy, "but what if they catch us?"

"Then we get in trouble," Sally said, "but that is okay."

They got to the next landing and froze at the door in front of them. Sally went for it and pushed down the handle, but the door was locked. She tried again and again but it wouldn't budge. She looked through the frosted glass but could see nothing distinct behind it, nothing but shadows.

Then, they heard from downstairs, the first floor landing door open. They froze, listened intently as they heard feet on stairs. Were they getting louder, or quieter? Was it someone coming up or down?

"We're stuck!" Jimmy said, his voice rising to a higher pitch as they both realized the person or people were coming up.

"No," Sally said, looking at the locked door, as the footsteps got louder. "We have to be calm."

"But…" Jimmy started as someone appeared on the landing, a woman in a tight smart skirt and a white blouse, looking at them suspiciously.

"Hi," the women said, "what are you guys doing here?"

Sally didn't say anything. She looked at Jimmy and could see he was shaking. She knew she was going to have to lie, but knew she was no good at it. *You have to meet her eye.* She thought.

"I said, what are you two doing up here?" The women said again, her expression hardening.

Meet her eye! Sally thought again.

"Did you hear me?" She asked.

"We have an appointment with George Farrington but we can't get through this door," Sally said, eyes resting on this women eyes, her legs feeling un-steady.

"Okay. Did Tim down on reception not show you up?" The woman asked, cocking her head to one side.

"No. He said the door would not be locked," Sally said.

"So, what's your appointment about?"

"My boyfriend Jimmy got a letter saying to come in when he had got experience so that he could do work."

"Oh, you mean work experience? Yeah, I heard they were doing some sort of program here. Why didn't you say?"

"Because we are both very nervous and have autism," Sally said, feeling strange as she said it. Strange but somehow good. Better then she had done talking to people before. And even though it was Jimmy's day and his moment she, for the first time was able to say, 'My name is Sally Hummel and I have autism.' And felt liberated, free and happy as she did.

"Oh. Okay, I didn't know that it was a program for people like you guys. But I guess that's PC now. Come on, I'll show you through."

"Thank you," Sally said, beaming, inside and out. "Thank you for helping us."

The women unlocked the door by scanning the barcode on her name badge that she wore around her neck and they were in.

"Is he expecting you?" She asked.

"Yes," Sally said.

"Right then, I can leave you to it. His office is the fourth on the right. Can you find that okay?"

"Yes," Sally said.

"Good," she said, and went through a door on their left.

"Come on Jimmy," Sally said, taking up his hand once more, when they were alone. "We're nearly there."

But Jimmy wouldn't move.

"I want to go home now," he said, looking down the long corridor towards the door.

"No," Sally said.

"But we should go home."

"We will not go home."

"Why? It's no good, I'm not going to ever work in films," Jimmy said, turning to go back the way they came.

"But…" Sally started.

"We should go back to the trains," Jimmy said, taking a few steps towards the door.

"No!" Sally said, grabbing him and pulling him back.

"But…" Jimmy tried.

"Jimmy, you are meant to be a film maker. And we have autism but we are still good at things and if we are good at things we do them. And you see mistakes in films and wouldn't make mistakes and work cameras and you care and we should do it. And you can do anything 'cos you make me feel like I can, that is amazing and I love you and we are doing this."

Jimmy looked at her, up and down, looked at the girl he loved and felt a surge of warmth run though him, warming him, calming him, focusing him.

If a girl as amazing as Sally loved him, then he could do anything. And if she thought he could do it…He thought… then he could.

His legs unfrozen, he took a few steps towards the office the lady had pointed out. Then a few more. Then suddenly he was pacing so quick that Sally could barely keep up with him, all the way to the brown door with George Farrington's name embossed upon it in gold and silver lettering.

Jimmy knocked on the door with three loud and deliberate thuds.

"Come in," a deep voice, bordering on gruff called.

"Okay," Jimmy called back and let go of Sally's hand.

"Good luck," she whispered softly as he went opened the door. "I'll be here."

"Okay," said Jimmy and went on inside.

Inside was a large modern office with pictures all around the walls, tiles underfoot partially covered by a plush, red and gold rug and a large, wooden desk with two laptops and a desktop computer on top.

George himself was a man of about forty, with hair too dark for his age, trendy glasses, wearing a navy suit and orange tie.

"Can I help you?" He said, looking up at Jimmy.

"Hi," Jimmy said, pooling his concentration to stop his voice from cracking, "my name is Jimmy Tiffin. You wrote me a letter saying about needing experience to get a job here," he said, holding up the letter. "And I have got experience by doing filming of an activity event at club and I have got this and you should look at it and then I could have a job doing filming?"

"Okay..." Said George, stumped for words for once. Most people understood that those letters were standard; he'd never had to explain further than this. "Now then young man, how did you get up here?"

"We should watch the film now," Jimmy said, taking a step forward towards the desk, brandishing his camera.

"Right, now I'm very busy Jimmy, I've got a lot of work to do. You can't come and see me without an appointment. Now as for getting a job here, we are fully staffed. We have all the people we need. I've pressed a button so security can come and show you out now."

"But if you watch the film…"

"I'm afraid this is not the way it works, Jimmy. You send in your CV, I invite you in, *then* we could watch the film."

"I have sent you my CV," Jimmy said, feeling tears of frustration begin to well, "you said get experience and so I did at club."

"Jimmy, I'm sorry, but you're going to have to leave. Security will be here soon."

"But I am good at filming…"

"Jimmy, life isn't that easy…"

"But I want a job in filming!" Jimmy shouted, not realizing he was doing so.

"We are fully staffed at the moment," George said, slowly and carefully.

"But…" Jimmy started.

"You need to apply to other places."

"But…" Jimmy tried again, just as the door was opened by a security guard followed by another.

"Right…" The first security guard said, putting his hand on Jimmy's shoulder.

"But…I don't want to work with your films anyway!" Jimmy shouted. "Your films are bad films. Like in the film with the men fighting in the field and the man gets shot in the arm but then the blood comes out his other arm. Or when they have the fight in the car park and the man had a watch on then the watch disappears or when he blows up the window and glass cuts him on the cheek and then it changes… or…" Jimmy tried as he was pulled out the room by the two men… "and when he rides the horse down the street and the barrel is on the wrong side of the road…" He shouted as the door was closed and he and Sally were half-led/half-dragged down the stairs, out the front entrance and pushed out the doors back onto the streets.

Jimmy looked back as the door was closed, then leant his head back and screamed; forcing his anger, his frustration, his disappointment and his shattered dreams out though his vocal cords and into the world around him so that it could know how he was feeling. Then he lifted the camera he had cherished for so many years, the object he'd always seen as his ticket, containing hours of footage, hours of films, good memories, good friends; lifted it above his head and threw it into the road where him and Sally watched it smash into eleven pieces, broken forever. People passing in the street looked at him, at them and shook their heads.

"Poor disabled guys," someone said knowingly to their friend, "I work with people like that, so I can tell. It's just that they don't understand, they don't mean to do things like that."

But Jimmy knew just what he was doing.

It was all so pointless.

II

"Why?" Jimmy asked for the twelfth time.

"Because, because we need to," Sally said for the twelfth time.

"But I don't understand," said a genuinely bewildered Jimmy. "We're not going to get jobs anyway."

"But we need jobs," said an increasingly frustrated Sally.

"But we won't get jobs," Jimmy said, looking out the window of the 231 bus as it slowed down to let people on.

Sally didn't answer for a couple of reasons. Mostly because it was pointless, he'd left his spark and his ambition at Showdown studios. It was hard enough getting him out of their bed this morning, let alone making him excited about the prospect of a cold afternoon job hunting in yet another town. But also because she knew the chances of them finding a job were, well… not good. But as she kept telling herself, she was an adult. And adults had jobs, it's what they did. They went to work every morning and came home in the evening and they earn money so that they could spend it on the things that they wanted.

"I want to go home," Jimmy said quietly to the window. "I want to go home and watch TV and go to bed."

"Oh," Sally said quietly. "Please can we go do looking for jobs?"

"I want to go home," Jimmy said again.

"Okay," Sally said softly, "we will go home."

Back at home they sat in the living room with Robert and Lilly and watched a documentary on wrestling that Robert had put on.

Jimmy curled himself up on the sofa, resting his hand on his head.

"Why is it so hard?" He asked the room.

No one answered. They didn't know. They knew it wasn't going to be easy for them, but they never imagined it would be this hard.

"It shouldn't be this hard," Duncan said from the doorway in which he'd been standing. "Maybe we should all go into business together, buy up a café and run it, so everyone can work?"

"Yeah, that would be good!" Sally said looking up at him.

"We just don't have that sort of money," Duncan said. "We'll win the lottery and then do it, eh?"

"Yes," said Robert, "let's win the lottery."

The house phone rang and Duncan went to answer it, leaving the four to watch the wrestling documentary in silence.

"Are we going to go to the club later on?" Lilly asked.

"No, not today," Sally said. "I am too tired to go do dancing."

"Oh, okay then. But I would like to see Kyle though, he is very nice, I like seeing Kyle."

"Yes, Kyle is very nice," Sally said, glad to be on a happier conversation. "We could run a café though, we would be very good."

"It costs a lot of money," said Jimmy. "We have to win the lottery."

"Right guys," Duncan said coming back in, "are you all going to club tonight?"

"I would like to," Lilly said, "to see Kyle."

"Well why don't we have Kyle round here? We could all stay in and watch a film, order some pizzas. It would be a good chance for you to meet a new support worker who may be working with you guys when I have my holiday away."

"Okay," Lilly said, "I will phone him and tell him that he can come round."

"Sounds good," said Duncan grinning at the prospect, "sounds very good."

"I don't want to watch a film," said Jimmy.

"Come on mate," Robert said, "don't let them bring you down!"

"Yeah, come on Jimmy, it would be nice," Sally said.

"There's this new one I really want to see, one you all haven't seen before," Duncan said. "I'm getting the support worker to bring it round."

"Okay," said Jimmy, "I will watch a film."

The new worker came around at eight, a tall thin man with trendy glasses who came in carrying a folder, a couple of bottles of coke and the DVD they were planning on watching.

"Hi, my name is Karl, how do you do?" He asked the group.

"Hello, my name is Lilly and this is my house and I live with my friends," Lilly said, shaking his hand excitedly, always enjoying meeting new people.

"How do we do what?" Sally asked him.

"Umm," Karl started, looking to Duncan.

"He just means hi," Duncan said to Sally.

"Oh. Hi," Sally said.

Karl came and sat with them on the sofa and Robert ordered the pizzas from their local takeaway restaurant with just a bit of help from Duncan.

"So, how long you been living here guys?" Karl asked the others.

"Nine months and five days," Sally answered.

"And do you like it here Jimmy?"

"Yes, I like the house," Jimmy said quietly. "What film are we going to watch?"

"We're gonna watch 'Old Trip,' it's a new one that's just come out. Have you seen it?"

"No," said Jimmy."

"Good, I didn't want to bring you guys one you'd seen. It's a comedy about some middle aged people who try and re-live their youths by going on the adventure holiday they went on in their gap years after university. Duncan tells me you want to work in films?"

"Yes. But I cannot do working in films as they won't let me."

"Oh, that's a shame," Karl said nodding. "Well, we can still enjoy the film eh? I hope it's a good one without too many mistakes."

"I like films but I don't like it when they get things wrong. It makes it bad," Jimmy said.

"Okay, well you'll have to tell me what you think of this one," Karl said. "Tell me whether it's good or not, that'd be okay?"

"Okay," said Jimmy, "I can do that."

"Yes, we can do that as we all watch films," Lilly said.

Kyle arrived at eight and the pizzas came shortly after. Once everyone had a slice in front of them, they put the film in the player. Karl had sat himself between Jimmy and Robert on the sofa, Sally sat at Jimmy's feet leaning against his legs, Lilly and Kyle on the arm chairs, Duncan cross legged on the floor next to the pizza and soft drinks which he served onto people's plates or into glasses when they needed it. The film started and straight away Jimmy got drawn into it, the opening credits started rolling and he felt that same excitement that he always did, which just hurt all the more when he thought how he'd never work in films.

They all thought the film was funny. Robert and Kyle especially were laughing most of the way through and Lilly and Sally spent much of the time chuckling. Karl kept asking questions, making the effort, especially with Jimmy.

"So, was that last scene okay?" He'd ask.

"Yes," Jimmy would answer, "it was very funny with the bit when they went into the sea and got bitten by the jelly fish."

Or he'd say: "No, the man lit the cigarette and then it is not lit." Or "The phone is in his wrong hand," and Karl didn't seem to mind. Most people got irritated if Jimmy spoke through the whole thing, but Karl seemed interested which made Jimmy happy.

When the film was over, Karl went into the kitchen to make a quick call and the others started clearing up.

"Shall we do watching another film?" Sally asked.

"No thank you, I will go to bed now," Jimmy said.

"Come on Jimmy! Let's watch a film!" Robert called, gesturing with his arms, just as Karl came back into the room, rubbing his hands together.

"Right then," he said to the assembled group who stopped what they were doing to listen.

"Are you going to do being our support worker?" Lilly asked, this usually being the point where they arranged the next time to meet.

"Actually, no," Karl said. "Sorry, you guys have been a bit tricked. I phoned Duncan to arrange all this. But I do have some good news, Jimmy," he said turning to the young man who was standing, bin bag in hand filling it with pizza boxes, "how would you like to come and work for Showdown pictures?"

"I would like to," said Jimmy, "but they wouldn't let me."

"Sorry mate," Karl said grinning now alongside Duncan who was positively beaming, "the thing was, Mr Farrington was so impressed by your knowledge of the mistakes, he wanted me to come and find out if it was things you'd read or whether you could just spot them easily. So I set up this with Duncan, kind of like an interview. And now, since you are so good at seeing mistakes, we'd like it if you would come and work for us on our new film as a continuity editor? So you'd come to our studio every day, watch what we are doing and tell us if there are mistakes so we can make sure we don't make any? The money's good and you'd be working with films…"

Jimmy's mouth dropped, his whole body tensed. He looked at Duncan, who was nodding and that was all the assurance he needed.

"That…that…that…" He stammered.

"That's amazing!" Sally shouted, jumping up and down on the spot.

"You did it you are going to be a film man and work in films!" Lilly shouted.

"Yes!" Robert shouted, grabbing Jimmy's shoulders.

Jimmy just stared and stuttered, unable to think, it had all seemed so hopeless and now… now he'd made it. He was going to be a film man. He'd done it!

He felt a tear run down his cheek and he started laughing at the same time, proper laughing from deep within him.

He'd made it.

He had made it.

Sally turned him around and they hugged for some time.

"I told you, you would do working in film," she said to him.

"Yes," said Jimmy. "I love you Sally."

"I love you too Jimmy," she told him. Amid this euphoric atmosphere, which even Karl couldn't help but feel well up inside him, Sally and Jimmy kissed again and both knew that they were going to be alright.

12

Jimmy was riding the train home from work on what was now a familiar route, watching out the window, his schedule for the journey and the day on paper in front of him, ticking off the stops as he went.

He got off at his stop, waved to Barbara the guard, who in turn blew him a kiss, then made his way down the station steps, two at a time.

Strolling slowly down the sun drenched high street he kept his head held high, smiling in any direction at all the other adults. He was an adult now, he understood that. But not just because he had a job, had his house and had his girlfriend. But because he understood himself and because he had become the person he wanted to be. It would still never be completely clear to him why people talked down to him, why they ignored him or thought he needed help all the time but he did know now that that was their problem and not his. He was happy, he had his friends, his job, his family, his house and best of all, his Sally. Who cared what anyone else thought or did?

He kept walking until he reached the café near the other end of the high street, just past a stationary shop and an old pub called The Ship.

"Jimmy!" Robert called from behind the counter once he'd gone inside. "How was the day?"

"It was my one year review day today," Jimmy said going up to his friend. "I am very tired, we are doing a film called 'The Other Island' it is okay. How is café?"

"The café is great! We have had many people in. It is been busy."

Jimmy looked around the café and indeed it was busy, eight of the twelve tables were in use; seven of them by people with disabilities with carers or family and one by people who'd wandered in off the street.

"That is good. Is Duncan happy?"

"Yes. We are making money so the funding people are happy that they do not have to fund anymore. And it is for respite and work experience. Duncan is happy."

"Good. Where is Sally?" Jimmy asked, as Robert poured him a latte from the loud machine.

"She is teaching Jane how to chop downstairs! That will be one pound please sir."

"Okay," said Jimmy opening his wallet. "Um… can you help me please?" He asked a hovering support worker who stepped forward and inspected the coins in Jimmy's wallet before finding a pound and giving it back to him to pay for the drink.

"Thank you."

"No problems Jim," the worker, who was wearing an apron which matched Robert's, said before going back to clearing the tables.

"I will call her on the phone to say you are here," Robert said. "Her work is nearly finished now. Mine is also. Julie is taking over with Helen and Dan."

"Okay," Jimmy said, "and then are we going to do parliament?"

"Yes. Yes we will go to parliament," Robert said. "Now please excuse me so I can serve this sir and madam," he added, nodding towards a young lady in a wheelchair and her support worker.

"Okay," Jimmy said taking a seat at the counter so he could wait for the others.

Their town's new learning disability parliament was held in the community centre and since the landslide victory; Lilly and Kyle were joint prime ministers of it. It was made up of seven adults with disabilities and although Jimmy, Robert or Sally weren't MPs they did come to help out when they could; making snacks for events, serving the drinks or giving short speeches on their experiences.

The parliament were currently planning a disability awareness day to be held at the town hall and Robert, Duncan and Sally were giving a speech about the café, how they had applied for government funding to set it up and had made it self sufficient. It was a real success story, marred only by the fact that they needed to go to those lengths just so that they could have jobs. Jimmy was also going to be talking about his job having become a minor celebrity due to his success.

"So we will do talking about services and then we will do guest speaker one and two and then we will do the mayor talking about what he is doing and then we will do the school teacher!" Lilly was saying, standing in front of the other MPs, her friends and a few support workers.

"Okay!" One of the other MPs said enthusiastically.

"And the café and drinks and snacks will be brought in by the café staff as they are very good at making food and people might get hungry and want to eat!" Lilly continued.

"Yeah," said Robert.

"Yes we will bring food," Sally said smiling at her best friend. "We will have pasta and sandwiches and Samosa's and salad."

"That is very good," said Kyle now standing up next to Lilly.

"Okay. We are nearly finished but before we have a drink we have to do saying a few announcements," Lilly said.

"Yeah, we want to say thank you!" Said Kyle, taking up his girlfriend's hand.

"Yes we would," Lilly started. "I would like to do saying thank you to our support workers. And for Robert for talking about being a coffee server at the event and Sally for cooking and Jimmy for being a film man and I would like to say congratulations to Jimmy and Sally who got engaged and will be doing getting married!"

Everyone turned to look at the seated couple, who turned to each other and kissed, sparking off a round of applause, wolf whistles and cheers.

"We cannot wait for the wedding!" Lilly added. "I will be maid of honor and it will all be amazing!"

Made in the USA
Charleston, SC
24 May 2011